TANGLED DESTINY

A Christmas Novella

OF GOLD & BLOOD
BOOK FOUR

Jenny Wheeler

Published by Happy Families Ltd

ISBN
978-1-99-117253-2 (Hardback)
978-0-473-45984-0 (Paperback)
978-0-473-45985-7 (E-Pub)
978-0-473-45986-4 (Kindle)
978-0-473-45987-1 (PDF)
978-0-473-45988-8 (iBook)

OF GOLD & BLOOD SERIES

Poisoned Legacy Book One
Brother Betrayed Book Two
Double Jeopardy Book Three
Tangled Destiny Book Four (Christmas novella and Prequel)
Unbridled Vengeance Book Five
Of Gold & Blood Boxed Set/Book Bundle Books 1 - 3

"But then, there is no satisfaction?"
"No satisfaction whatever, at any time," she cried passionately. "There is only a queer divine dissatisfaction, a blessed unrest, that keeps us marching and makes us more alive than the others."

— Martha Graham to Agnes De Mille, quoted *in Martha, The Life and Work of Martha Graham*, Random House, 1991.*

*Thanks to Jane Ellen, of the Glistening Particles Podcast, for bringing the Martha Graham quote to my attention.

One

December 6, 1847

"To the belle of the ball — Elanora! Happy birthday, my dear daughter!" Her father's normally embittered face carried a faint, benign smile that she'd seldom seen since her mother's death two years ago. He reached for his lemonade glass and raised it in a toast.

"May the coming years bring you all the happiness you deserve."

She glanced from her father's wheelchair to the man standing an arm's length away. If she reached out, she could take his hand in hers. She resisted the impulse.

The happiness her father wished for her, that she hoped for, all rested in his lithe, muscular form, with the quicksilver mobile face that responded to everything around him, the startling aquamarine eyes and long-fingered expressive hands that were seldom at rest. An artist's hands, out of place juggling import and export files.

Eustace Reverdy Mountfort, twenty-three, the man she'd been secretly hoping would "pop the question" on this milestone night of her twenty-first birthday. They'd been whispering of it for months, and she'd been certain he'd recognize the significance of the occasion tonight, would take the opportunity to ask her to be his wife. As of tonight, didn't she step into some degree of autonomy, as well as a comfortable inheritance from her maternal grandfather?

She caught his eye, and he shot her a look of longing that made her heart bang against her ribs. She moved her hand surreptitiously to rest under her breasts, holding herself in check, calming her restless hope. It certainly wouldn't do to let anyone see how she felt. Rather, she made a deferent bob of her head towards Henry Travers. "Thank you, Father."

Henry inclined his head toward Eustace. "Obviously I am not capable of taking up the honor of dancing with my daughter on this Coming-Of-Age occasion, more's the pity. Eustace, can I ask you to stand in for me?"

Eustace smiled and bowed — a semi-mocking, good-natured swoop from the waist. "With great pleasure." His voice rumbled within her chest cavity, setting off another wave of trembling as he stepped towards her and offered her his arm. "Elanora Grayson Travers, would you do me the honor of the first post-dinner dance?"

Twenty-five of the Travers' family's closest friends and relatives had gathered for this St Nicholas night birthday celebration in Broadway's luxurious Rainbow Restaurant, famous for welcoming ladies through its doors when many other establishments still only permitted men to dine.

They'd supped on smoked salmon and crème brulee on gold plates which reflected sparkling light from walls lined with gilded mirrors. With the marble floors, elaborate ceiling scroll work and richly upholstered seats, visitors were put in mind of the excesses of Versailles, and the Rainbow had been a sensation ever since opening.

At one end of the restaurant was a dancefloor equipped with a ten-piece orchestra, so guests could end the night with a waltz. Eustace and Elanora had made one circuit of the floor when she felt a tap on her shoulder, and Eustace's warm reassuring arm at her waist tensed into rigid constraint.

"I'm sure my son is happy to allow fleeting youth to accede to wisdom." The words were jocular, but the tone was determined and humorless. William Mountfort's six-foot-four frame loomed over them as his son shuffled aside.

"Of course, Father." The hooded pleading of the sea green eyes didn't need translation: *Humor him. Please.*

Eustace's father had bestowed upon his son his virile good looks and military bearing, but the younger's winsome charm was completely lacking in the senior. The barrel chest, the iron-willed stance of his tree-trunk thighs, and the bulldog dewlaps that hung either side of his chin, all communicated at a glance William Perrin Mountfort's drive to dominate at any cost.

He grasped Elanora tightly and expertly propelled her into a dizzying series of twirling spins which left her feeling slightly nauseous.

He settled back into a more sedate rhythm and gave her a slow self-satisfied smile, happy to have stamped his control. "You're looking particularly ravishing tonight, young Elanora." He raised a strong arching brow in a query. "Not for anyone's particular benefit, I hope?"

She flushed at his ham-fisted insensitivity. William Mountfort was famous for his indifference to other people's feelings, especially those of his long-suffering wife Connie, her beloved Aunt Coco.

Although she should have been fully prepared for his bumptious nosiness, she felt a hot temper rising. "I'm really not sure what you mean, Mr Mountfort. I think it's generally recognized a girl wants to look her best on her twenty-first birthday. Wouldn't you agree?"

"Of course, my dear, of course." He slowed his dance steps and drew her more closely to him. She could smell the after-dinner cognac on his breath and suppressed a shudder.

"However, I wouldn't like a beautiful young woman like you to have her heart broken." His steel gray eyes slid over her, cool assessment rather than concern clearly mirrored there.

"Now you really are talking in riddles."

Her voice was over bright and too sharp to sound casual. She gave a throaty laugh. "And at twenty-one, I really am too old for guessing games."

She gave her best display of amused bewilderment. "Why don't you just come right out and tell me what's concerning you. I'm sure I'll be able to set your worries to rest."

There. The challenge had been issued. And didn't she know better than to challenge William Mountfort on anything? The way she'd seen him treat Connie, who'd been nothing but a dedicated compassionate wife over many years, should have taught her that.

William Mountfort stopped dancing. He was a technically expert dancer, so the sudden arresting of his fluid movement brought them to an abrupt stop. He gazed down at her with a look far removed from fatherly concern and offered her his arm with a decisiveness which could not be defied.

"It's rather warm in here with all those gas heaters at floor level. Let's take a turn along the pergola."

As she hesitated, he hooked her right arm over his and strolled towards the doors onto the enclosed terrace that adjoined the restaurant. The promenade lights accentuated the sinuous lines of grape branches that entwined the pillars — bare now in December, but promising green fruitfulness in late summer.

As they walked, he spoke in a low measured tone, pitched exactly for her ears alone. "What I'm about to say is very much for your own good, Miss Travers. A father's heart, and all that." He glanced down at her with his cold assessing eyes.

"Let's just say I would be concerned if you had any thoughts of setting your very lovely blond head in my son's direction." He glanced down at her again, as she fought to continue the nonchalant strolling, while inside she locked up in shock.

"If that were the case, I have to warn you, you'll be waiting a very long time. Eustace is ill-prepared for any commitments other than learning the family business right now, and he understands that very well."

He gave her another calculating look. "There is a great deal he needs to learn before he will be ready to take over the reins of Mountfort Imports, and I'm sure you understand that must be his first priority." He paused and turned to face her. "I just didn't want there to be any misunderstandings about his situation."

Her tongue felt as locked down as the rest of her, but she knew she had to speak. She licked her lips, cleared her throat and flashed him her best fake smile.

"A father's heart. I do so appreciate your concern, Mr Mountfort." She was practically purring.

"I'm just not sure why you don't consider Eustace capable of working in the business as well as maintaining a family life. After all, I believe that's exactly what you did at his age, is it not? Aunt Coco has often talked about those early years when you were establishing the business and Eustace was just a baby."

She smiled again. "Not that I have any 'intentions' as you so delicately put it. Eustace and I have been good friends for a long time, as you know. But that's the beginning and end of it."

She met his implacable stare with one of bland surprise and held his gaze until he looked away and resumed the stroll.

They walked in silence for a minute or longer, and then Mountfort spoke again. "Thank you Elanora. I find your response reassuring, I really do, because it's my intention to broaden Eustace's commercial experience by sending him to the West Indies for a couple of years.

"He understands he needs to get away from his mother's indulgence and learn a few lessons in the school of hard knocks. It will make a man of him. And I don't consider the West Indies any place for a wife."

She stopped walking, withdrawing her arm from his as she halted. "I'm not sure why the Indies is 'no place for a wife'. I imagine myriads of women raise families there. But let me assure you, it's not on the top of my list of places to visit."

She drew herself up to her full five-foot-four height and glared up at him. "Now if you'll excuse me, I really had better get back to the rest of my guests."

As she turned to stride away, she got a fleeting glimpse of the gloating satisfaction that crossed his face as he said, "Of course. Don't let me detain you any longer."

His father was such an ass. Eustace Reverdy Mountfort sighed and glanced around the room for the umpteenth time to check if Elanora and William had returned. It was so typical of his father to ride roughshod over everyone else to get what he wanted. And he had a niggling sense of dread about his father's intentions.

The glass door from the terrace to the reception room gusted open and Elanora stood in the entry, backlit by the terrace lights, like an angel, in a frothy pink lace-trimmed dress that sat breathtakingly low on her shoulders.

She glanced around the room and her eyes flashed as they settled on him. He knew that look. She was furious. She stood like a queen on the boundary of her realm, awaiting her retainers, and he braced himself as he stalked toward her.

When he got closer he saw that below her fury she was deeply hurt. He melted inside. If there was one thing he hated more than any other, it was seeing her upset.

"What is it?" He spoke softly as he stood before her. She hated public displays, he knew that, but he sensed that whatever it was that was eating at her couldn't wait.

She drew him to one side out of the doorway, and they sank onto a bench seat backing onto the wall. "When were you going to tell me you're going to the West Indies for years? Is that something you just happened to overlook?"

She was fingering a lace handkerchief and her hands were trembling. When she looked up her eyes were narrowed with pain.

"Do I mean so little to you that you forgot to mention it?"

Her lower lip trembled but she held her head high.

"Oh, my darling. It's something he's just got a bee in his bonnet about. And I've been hoping either Mother or I could change his mind …" His voice trailed off into silence. He sounded so weak and indecisive, but it was so hard to stand up to William Mountfort.

He glanced around the room, then reached out and took her hand in his. It felt like a little bird, small and fragile. "Elanora, we need a chance to talk in private. Not here. It's important. I'll explain —"

He let go of her hand and glanced around the room again. He could see Elanora's father, his mother, even her Aunt Glory, looking their way; they were starting to notice her absence. Heads were turning.

"We can't talk now. But we have to do it later tonight. Promise me."

Two

The tip of his nose was icy as he took her in his arms and buried his face in her hair, but the rest of him was warm, so warm. She relaxed and let herself enjoy the closeness, the slightly stuffy smell of his worsted jacket and carbolic soap.

It was the smell of Eustace, going right back to their school days, when they'd attended different schools suited to their education — him as one born to rule, her as one to reign at home — and they'd only been able to see one another during school holidays when their families met.

With a pang she wondered if this would be one of the last days she'd be able to lean close and breathe in the tangible memory of him. He couldn't really be going away for years, could he?

She pulled back and patted his hair, which was damp with snowflakes. "Come into the library. It's still warm in there. I've built the fire up again."

For the last hour of her party, she'd been barely aware of what was happening around her while playing at being the courteous, pliable birthday girl, an heiress with a modest legacy and uncertain prospects. Only a couple of hours later, and it already seemed like the party had been for someone else.

Eustace had kept his promise and had waited down the street until the house lights dimmed and it was clear her father had been put to bed and the servants retired. Then he'd tapped softly on the library window as arranged and she'd let him in.

She proudly gestured to the hot chocolate she'd brewed that sat cooling on a tray; if a woman's job was to create a nurturing home, she was showing him she could excel at it.

They'd barely sunken into the armchairs either side of the fire before she whispered urgently to him, "So tell me. What's happening? You're not really going away for years, are you?"

The joy in his face drained away. The desperation of a hunted quarry took its place.

"Elanora, I don't know. I don't want to go. Mother definitely doesn't want me to go — she is totally opposed to the idea. But my father seems set on it. You know what he's like. When he gets fixed on something he won't let it go."

"So what will you do then? If he is determined on it?"

He gazed into her eyes. The fire hissed and spat. The mantle clock chimed two. He shook his head. "I don't know, Ellie. I just don't know. This is what I'm born to do. To inherit the family business. I've never considered doing anything else. I don't know that I'm suited to do anything else ..."

He picked nervously at a loose thread on his jacket, his eyes pleading for understanding.

"You know I want to be able to provide well for my family — our family — and going into business with Father is undoubtedly the best way to do that."

Her heart lurched at the mention of the future they may not now be able to share.

"Do you really think we can be apart for two — maybe three — years and still make it all work out?"

The words were barely a whisper. She knew she wanted him to assure her that of course they could. And she knew in her heart of hearts she'd be a fool to believe him.

He set his hot chocolate down and slid across to nestle on the arm of her chair. He put his arm around her neck and drew her to him, slipping in beside her as he did and drawing her onto his lap, so she was completely encircled in his arms.

"Ellie, you are all I want. I would wait till the Last Days for you." His voice was raw and tender. He breathed in her ear and nibbled around the lobe. "I love you to China and back. The Indies? I think we can handle that."

His eyes were fervent as he gazed into her face, and then he leaned in and kissed her, gently at first and then with a building passion.

"Will you marry me, Elanora Travers?" He cupped her face in his hands and kissed her eyelids. "Marry me, please ... I will have no other." He blew gently on her face. "No other, do you hear?"

He slipped his hand into his jacket pocket and drew out a black velour-covered jeweler's box, which he slowly opened before her. A gorgeous antique diamond ring sparkled in the firelight. "And to prove it ..."

He drew the ring from the nest of blue tissue paper and held it up for her to see. She stretched out her left hand, and he slid the precious circle onto her ring finger, caressing her palm as he did.

When it was set in place, he took the hand tenderly between his own, turned it over and peppered the delicate skin with butterfly kisses, progressing up her arm, feathering it with his warm lips. Before she recognized what was happening, he had his hand under her skirts, and she didn't object.

Her dream had come true. Eustace had asked her to marry him. They were betrothed on her twenty-first birthday as she'd dreamed they would be. That meant everything was going to be just fine from now on, didn't it?

When she slipped to the door an hour later to send Eustace home before the household awoke, she told herself she was Mrs Eustace Mountfort in everything but name. She clung to him momentarily as he drew her close and gave her one, two, three passionate farewell kisses. How cruel that they had to be separated for even a few hours. Soon though, they would be together forever.

As she watched Eustace's back disappearing into the faintly purple dawn light, his head ringed with vapor clouds from his hot breath in the icy air, she shot a desperate arrow prayer heavenwards.

Please God, help Connie make William understand.

She and Eustace were to be together 'till death do us part'. And as far as she was concerned, their wedding couldn't come soon enough.

Three

It was the tiny two-foot-tall General Tom Thumb who turned Elanora Travers and her school friend Amelia Jackson from warm acquaintances to the sharers of a secret that Elanora wished she'd never known.

The brilliant star of PT Barnum's Broadway freak show stole Amelia's heart during an indulgent afternoon spent trailing through the great showman's American Museum, being amused by a diorama of Napoleon's funeral and numerous other curiosities: midgets, giants, albinos, educated dogs and industrious fleas, ventriloquists and automatons.

According to Phineas Barnum these, along with a hundred other eccentricities, were "exceedingly successful" in making his the most popular show in the city.

Elanora might have preferred to stay and watch the fancy glass-blowing, but when Amelia set eyes on General Tom Thumb, working the stage like a lively animated doll, blond hair framing a perfectly round face, swinging his cane and mounting his tiny 'walnut' carriage drawn by Shetland ponies, Amelia closed off any further discussion by bursting into tears.

And that's when it occurred to Elanora that Amelia had been unusually quiet in the hour they'd already spent browsing the exhibit halls. She'd been far too preoccupied by the astounding events of last night in her father's library to pay her much attention.

She blushed at the memory of Eustace, of his hands, his mouth, and she glanced self-consciously at her left hand. It was bare, the diamond ring hidden in her dresser drawer.

She'd promised Eustace that until he'd cleared their engagement with his father she would not speak of it to anyone, but it was a secret that burned through her skin and she imagined even singed through the bodice of her blue velvet day dress.

Truth was, she felt strangely disconnected from her surroundings, as if her real life as Mrs Eustace Mountfort was already hidden from view, but taking form in the wings. Soon she'd step onto center stage and take up her leading role. Currently she was just a lady-in-waiting.

Amelia snuffled a very unladylike snort

into her damp shoulder, and she dropped back down to earth with a thump. "Amelia … Amelia. What is it? Don't be so upset. There's nothing to cry about."

She stroked her friend's hair consolingly. The General had returned to the stage in country yokel overalls to sing a selection of patriotic songs in a high sweet voice.

Amelia gave a violent shake of her head and hissed back. "You don't know. You've no idea." Her body shook with suppressed sobbing.

Right. Elanora glanced around her, thankful to see no one in the hundred-strong audience seemed in the least interested in their mini drama. All eyes were riveted on General Tom, their whispers drowned out by thunderous applause.

She made a snap decision. "Let's find

somewhere quiet for you to recover. Come on." She drew her arm around her friend's neck and cossetted her out of the gallery, their heads hanging close together like two young women exchanging girlish secrets. The looming arched entryway of St Paul's chapel beckoned from across the street.

What better place for private confessions than a church? In a few minutes they'd dodged the carriages and crowds that were a perpetual feature of this section of Broadway and were nestled on a back bench in sacred peace of the old church.

"There we are. Now take a deep breath. Dry your eyes and tell me what's wrong."

She gave her friend a sympathetic smile and sat back and waited.

"You won't understand. You'll think I'm

terrible." Tears welled up in Amelia's eyes and spilled over to run silently down her cheeks. Her friend's normally bright expression was slack, her eyes wet and dull.

Elanora took one of her hands and squeezed it. "No, I won't. We all do silly things sometimes. I'm sure it's nothing too awful."

Amelia regarded her in fearful silence. "No one does something this awful."

"Why did General Tom set you off so? He's a very successful performer — and they say a very wealthy young man. What's so sad about that?"

Amelia gave a deep shuddering sigh. "You don't understand. It's what he reminds me of ... that sweet baby face ..."

Elanora's heart was clutched by a sudden. impossible, icy thought. "Amelia, you're not ... you're not in the family way, are you?"

She needed no words of confirmation. Amelia covered her face in her hands and talked through her fingers in heaving sobs. Elanora only heard incoherent snatches. "I don't know … No one to turn to … I can't believe … this mess."

Elanora drew a fresh, neatly ironed handkerchief out of her purse and pushed it gently into Amelia's hands. "It's not the end of the world. He'll just have to marry you, that's all."

Amelia burst into the loudest wailing yet. "I can't … I can't do that. He's already married."

"Oh, you poor girl. You poor, poor girl." She drew her friend to her shoulder and let her sob herself to quiet exhaustion. Then she patted her cheeks dry and stroked her arms. "Come on, Amelia. There must be something we can do. Has he got means?

"The least he can do is ensure you can go somewhere nice and quiet till your confinement. Well, you know what I mean. No, now, don't start crying again. That won't get you anything except a blotchy puffed-up face."

Amelia's throat caught in a hiccupping laugh. Elanora goaded her friend on. "We couldn't have that now, could we?" Their wan laughter echoed around the stone chamber. "Shhhsshhh." The silly admonition — often used by the French teacher at their private girl's school — set them off in fresh giggles.

"Good. Now you're feeling better, let's work out a plan. Firstly, honor bound, tell me who this cad is. I promise I won't …"

Before the sentence was out, Amelia was shaking her head violently and looking like she'd burst into fresh tears. "Elanora I can't …"

"Oh, for goodness sakes, of course you can. You didn't get to this place alone." Elanora's voice was bossy and decisive. "He has responsibilities."

Amelia looked at her speculatively. "You're not going to like it."

For a fraction of a second, she thought of Eustace, and then just as instantly realized he wasn't married. Yet. She let out a long sigh of relief.

"Honestly, Amelia, I have no particular allegiances. Don't be afraid."

Amelia gazed at her for a long, considering moment.

"Alright then."

She glanced around her as if checking for eavesdroppers and then leaned very close to her ear and whispered, "It's your paramour's father. William Perrin Mountfort."

Four

His mother did not look well. Constanza sat at one end of the gleaming walnut dining table in a burnt orange gown which drained the color from her sallow complexion and left her looking tired and depleted. The mesh of fine wrinkles that hugged her eyes did not look like laughter lines — although when she was in good spirits, Connie laughed a lot.

Eustace fiddled with the silver knife at his elbow and restrained himself from glancing to the door, where he anticipated at any minute Elanora would be ushered in, pushing her father ahead of her.

His heart beat a tattoo in his chest

whenever he allowed himself to savor the thought, the taste, of her and of the passionate connection they'd shared two nights ago. He adored her, desired her body, soul and spirit.

And although he'd given her his troth, he had no idea how he was going to keep it, how he was going to circumvent his father's determination to send him off to Purgatory. Otherwise known as Barbados.

That's why his mother's downcast mood rattled him more than usual. Connie had always been his protector against his father's unbending will. Many a time she had stepped in and mediated William's harsh excesses, placated his insistence that the hard way was the only way.

However, since his twenty-first birthday nearly three years ago, Connie's moderating influence had waned. William had stopped taking notice of her, and he sensed his father was not going to be swayed from his determination to put him on the next boat out of New York, no matter how strongly his mother opposed the idea.

A fresh gust of chilled air whooshed into the stuffy overheated room, and his eyes went instantly to the door, where Elanora was entering, bending over, solicitous to her father, an angelic vision in a shimmering pale apricot gown which highlighted the light gold translucence of her skin.

She moved with grace, head bent towards her father to catch his words, then rising to her full height, all supple grace and smiles, a young beauty in full bloom.

She glanced across the room as if her

spirit was irresistibly drawn to his, and her cheeks flushed a faintly deeper gold as their eyes locked. They held that gaze, unaware of anyone else in the room for long seconds, and then with what he sensed was a steely control, she turned to his mother.

"Aunt Coco … We are so delighted to be here."

Their families had been friends since long before he and Elanora were born, and Connie — though no relation of blood in any way — had comforted Elanora with a mother's heart in the years since her own mother had died.

From a tiny tot Ellie had called Constanza 'Aunt Coco'. Connie would like nothing better than to weave her into their family as her daughter-in-law.

The two women shared a brief hug, and then Elanora parked her father in his chair alongside their hostess — the seat she always insisted be reserved for him — and shook hands with William before progressing down the table to take her place beside his fifteen-year-old sister Alycia.

Elanora patted her on the shoulder and leaned in and kissed her cheek. "Alycia, you are getting more grown up every day. In no time at all you'll be the belle of the ball!" He sensed his serious-minded young sister stiffening a little at the compliment.

She flashed Elanora a wry grin. "But I don't want to be belle of the ball!"

Elanora patted her arm affectionately. "Of course you do. Any girl of fifteen does." She turned to greet the diner on her left and missed the annoyance that flashed across Alycia's face.

Constanza cleared her throat and

nodded — Eustace's cue to act as heir apparent and welcome the guests to the table. He got to his feet, looking to William as he rose.

"Father," a nod of deference, "Mother," another pause, "and all our very welcome guests. We're gathered here together, as you know, to celebrate another very successful year for Mountfort Imports. Thanks to my father's astute direction, we have enjoyed our best year ever and look forward to an exciting new alliance in the year to come."

He turned to the white-haired man seated on his right and to the younger man with the same patrician profile who sat next to him. "We're delighted to have Mr James Wollander and his son Bartholomew with us tonight. Let me introduce you to the guests you haven't yet met."

He gestured to Elanora and Henry. "I think you know everyone here except Mr Henry Travers and his daughter Elanora, who are very close friends of our family."

Elanora bestowed a winning smile on the newcomers. "Delighted to meet you, I am sure. Forgive our late arrival." She glanced to her father's wheelchair. "Unavoidable sometimes, I'm afraid."

James Wollander's eyebrows rose in appreciation. "I'm sure your father is delighted to have such a devoted daughter, Miss Travers. So glad to make your acquaintance."

He glanced down at Eustace and back to Elanora. "We're very strong in the sugar trade in the Indies, and Eustace and William have excellent sales networks here and elsewhere. I can see us all working together very well."

He smiled around the table and the

other guests: Will Jackson, the company lawyer, and his wife Adelaide, and Mountfort accountant Sam Chambers and his spinster daughter Cassandra — visibly relaxed and looking expectantly to their plates. Eustace noticed for the first time this evening that Will and Adelaide Jackson's daughter Amelia, who often accompanied her parents to these functions, was absent.

"Thank you, Eustace. Formalities almost over. Time for grace!" William Mountfort chimed a teaspoon against a wine glass to get attention, recited a perfunctory prayer and black-aproned servants trailed in with first course: tureens of pea soup and platters of cold tongue.

"So, Elanora, my dear girl, what have you been doing with yourself since your wonderful birthday party?" Connie had put on gold-rimmed glasses and looked over them fondly.

Elanora paused with a spoonful of soup halfway to her mouth. "Oh, not a lot Aunt Coco. I went to Barnum's with Amelia the other day and we saw General Tom! That was an experience!"

Elanora flashed a smile at Amelia's mother. "Amelia isn't with us tonight — is she quite well?"

Adelaide nodded. "Perfectly well, thank you. Just needed to rest. She's been so busy lately."

Elanora glanced back to Connie. "General Tom's a remarkable little fellow — have you ever seen him?"

Constanza shook her head. "Oh no, dear, I'm far too busy." There was a satisfied silence as the guests cleaned up their plates ready for the next course, then William's voice chimed in, loud and intrusive.

"Looking after all the paupers in the municipality, aren't you, Constanza? Or as you like to call them the 'deserving poor'." The corner of William's mouth turned up in a sneer.

Eustace saw his mother's shoulders stiffen, but when she turned to answer him, her expression was composed.

"I know we don't see eye to eye on everything, William, but I'm sure there's room for more than one opinion in the most successful of marriages. That's what keeps them interesting, isn't it? However, our guests don't want to hear about it over dinner."

She fixed her calm gaze on him for a few more seconds and then smiled fleetingly at Elanora. "Now what were you just saying my dear? Barnum's circus is still drawing the crowds, then?"

"It certainly is."

Eustace sensed that beneath the gay rejoinder, something was troubling Elanora. And when he glanced back at his father, he could see he had not taken his wife's mild reprimand well. His face above his black beard was brick red, his jawline rigid.

As the main course rolled on — roast turkey, oyster pie, baked sweet potatoes, celery and squash — it became clear Mr James Wollander was much enamored with Miss Elanora Travers, and he exercised every gambit at his command to engage her in conversation, while his son sat mute beside him.

Which human curiosities had she enjoyed most at Barnum's? Where would she and her esteemed father be spending Christmas Day? And had she ever been to the West Indies?

"No, I have not, Mr Wollander. I

haven't traveled any farther than Saratoga, although one day I certainly would like to visit foreign climes."

She smiled encouragingly over her wine glass. "Have you been living in Bridgetown long? I suppose it's very hot most of the time? And I suppose there's lots of palm trees?"

"It is hot, Miss Travers, most assuredly. But you get used to it. And there are lots of palms, for sure. Barbados is known for them."

"Elanora won't need any palm trees. She's not going anywhere. It's Eustace who's going."

William had hardly spoken during the meal, and even Eustace was shocked by the surly undertone in his father's casual remark.

Wollander's neck flushed red above his collar.

"Oh, of course, Mr Mountfort. A silly remark. I meant nothing by it."

William dismissed the protest. "Not your fault, James. Not at all. It's just young people sometimes get silly ideas." He looked at Wollander junior, who seemed to shrink into his chair under his cool gaze.

"Possibly your young chap Bartholomew is the exception. But I was just wanting to make our arrangement quite clear. Eustace goes to work with you in your order and dispatch department, while Bartholomew comes to New York and learns our end of the business. When we agree the time is right we will discuss a merger of Mountfort and Wollander. Or Wollander and Mountfort."

He threaded his fingers and placed his hands in a satisfied gesture in front of his mounded belly.

"That's the only way the arrangement will work. And Eustace doesn't need any encumbrances to distract him from his work."

An awkward silence fell over the table. Eustace ventured a glance toward Elanora. She sat bolt upright, but head down, staring at the empty space where her plate had been, gripped by an icy composure. And she chewed her lip. A sure sign she was upset.

Constanza grasped the silver hand bell next to her wine glass and rang it vigorously. "Time for dessert, I think, and then the gentlemen can disperse for their cigars and liquor while we ladies enjoy a coffee." She looked to the door as it swung open at the butler's hand. "Oh, there you are, Mr O'Malley. We're ready for our Chancellor's Pudding with brandy sauce. Please serve it at once."

Eustace turned to Bartholomew Wollander, who looked nearly as mortified as Elanora. "You'll find New York rather different after Bridgetown. Have you spent much time here before?"

Bartholomew grasped at the thread gratefully. "No, not really. I did some of my schooling at Albany, but that was a while ago. And New York changes so fast. They reckon that even if you grow up here, move away for five years and you won't recognize the place when you get back."

He flashed an uncertain grin. "You might find that yourself. Not that you're going to be away five years of course. But you never know. You might get to really like the place."

Eustace glanced uneasily across the table to Elanora. She had lifted her head and was staring directly at him, her eyes wounded. She thrust up from her chair suddenly. "Aunt Coco, I'm so sorry, but I do seem to be developing a headache. Could I retire to the parlor and rest? I don't want to spoil the fun."

Constanza looked concerned. "You're not going to faint, dear girl? It wasn't those oysters?"

"No, no, I'm fine. Just got a nasty headache, that's all. Father, just call when you're ready to go home. No need to rush."

She turned toward the door, a stricken sheen on her cheeks. Eustace rose to follow. "Let me accompany you, Elanora. We wouldn't want you to fall."

Before he could escape from his chair, his father's lumberjack's hand thumped the table. "Leave the girl be, Eustace. Can't you see she wants some privacy? And you've got guests to entertain."

The Wollanders were silent. Will and Adelaide, and Sam and Cassandra were trying hard to not notice anything was amiss, chatting lightly among themselves, but Eustace knew the score.

His father had very publicly declared Elanora had no place in his future as the heir to the Mountfort Wollander enterprise. And unless he found some freakish way to escape, that commercial union was going to supercede any hope he had for personal nuptials with his beloved Ellie.

Five

Elanora slept with the little black box under her pillow that night, but it did nothing to ward off the crushing headache that throbbed at her temples when she woke in the early hours of the morning and lay staring into the dark dawn. Well, she'd learned one thing. An engagement ring in the little black box didn't have magic powers to make everything alright again.

So just how did she pick herself up and go on from here? She had been imagining herself sharing her life with Eustace since she was sixteen. She'd had only eyes for him since she'd had a nanny in the nursery. And she'd avoided seeing the thing that now stuck out more clearly than any other.

Eustace would never stand up to his father and be his own man. His comfortable life as merchant-man-about-town depended on him obeying his father's every wish. This week it was the demand that he goes to the Indies. This time next year it would be something else.

She rested her hand on her stomach and recalled their love making. All done on impulse, but on the assumption they were soon to be man and wife. She rolled over in bed, suddenly feeling hot and sweaty even though the snow still lay several feet deep on the ground outside. She drew her knees up to her chest and keened silently, rocking from side to side, a sharp stabbing pain in her chest.

She put her hands to her eyes and pressed them down so hard she saw little shards of light behind her fingers. How could she have been so naive? Didn't they say "Like father, like son?" She really should have known better, and nothing would ever be the same again.

Even with Aunt Coco. She pictured Coco's kind, careworn face, one she now knew better even than her own mother's. Things wouldn't be the same there either. Firstly, she knew William's awful secret.

How could she look Coco in the eye and not have something of what she knew leak out of her? And secondly, Coco's first loyalty would always have to be to her son. She, Elanora, was no longer in the first circle of family. She'd just been banished.

What to do? Who to talk to? She

couldn't imagine that her life would not be scarred forever by what had unfolded last night.

Unbelievably, she dropped off into the welcome oblivion of an exhausted sleep, and the light had fully broken when she was woken hours later by an urgent rapping on her bedroom door. She struggled up from the pillow and the hammering in her head resumed the second she opened her eyes. A bitterness burned in her mouth.

She recognized the Irish brogue of their housekeeper, Dana O'Loughlin; a doughty woman Aunt Coco had rescued from a Five Points tenement house and helped set back on her feet.

"Miss Elanora …" There was the faintest hint of a rolled "r" in the loving caress of her name. A long pause. "Miss Elanora, please … You have a visitor."

Her heart leapt. Eustace. It was Eustace coming to tell her he was choosing her over his father. That he was going to start work as … She flopped back onto the pillow. It was not going to be Eustace.

"Who is it, Dana?"

"Miss Amelia is here to see you. She says you were taken unwell last night, and she's concerned."

"That I was, Dana. That I was. But I'm better this morning. It was just a headache, nothing serious."

She drew her legs to the edge of the bed and placed them down on the rug that overlay the cold wooden floor. "Give me just a few minutes to clean up and I'll be down. Set her in the parlor and make some coffee, would you be so kind, Mrs O'Loughlin. I'll be down, right smart."

"Certainly miss. Straight away. Miss Amelia will be ever so relieved."

So Amelia's parents had reported last night's humiliation. The chill of the ice-cold water from the bedside ewer was just what she needed. She dipped and rung out the muslin face cloth and applied it to her eyelids, the back of her neck, her arm pits.

Then she doused herself in lavender water in the places where she'd had the ice-cold cloth. Within minutes she was pleasantly revived. She wasn't going to give anyone the satisfaction of talking about her behind her back. And today, what was it, a week before Christmas. She was going to set about making a new start.

Six

"This color would look wonderful on you!" Amelia stood beside a mahogany counter in Alexander Stewart's cavernous five-story Broadway department store and fingered a bolt of pale green and red striped alpaca — the hot new fabric for ladies' fashion. She smiled encouragingly. "You could put it together with that raspberry velvet for a mantle and that green bonnet lined with the rose-pink satin over there."

Elanora laughed at her friend's earnest eagerness. "I'm fine, really Amelia. I don't need to be spending any more of Father's funds."

Amelia reached out, her hands warm

through her thin kid gloves. "You deserve a Christmas treat. You're so devoted to him. And he can afford it. Why not lash out and buy a length for a new promenade dress? Give yourself a boost?"

They were on the second floor of A T Stewart's 'first department store in the world' — popularly referred to as the 'Marble Palace' because of its magnificent Italian Renaissance palazzo styling and dazzling white marble facade.

Elanora looked around her at the airy circular courtyard that stretched for the full height of the interior, covered by a domed skylight. They were only a few blocks from the wharves and the Mountfort's warehouses, but you felt you were in another protected, opulent world.

Since it had opened a year ago,

Stewart's was the only place to shop for the fashionable set. Some ladies even sat outside in their carriages and had merchandise brought out to them for their approval. Elanora and Amelia had come downtown in Amelia's father's carriage and were browsing the 'Ladies' Parlor' where they could admire themselves in full length Parisian mirrors.

Mannequin dummies displayed the season's 'look'. Every year it seemed skirts were getting bigger, the sleeves more cumbersome and the bodices tighter and harder to breathe in. They were dresses designed for women who did very little except sit passively and observe life passing them by.

Elanora shook her head. She felt bruised from last night's encounter with William Mountford. She could swear her ribs felt sore, and she didn't want to squeeze herself into a gown designed for graceful submissiveness. These dresses made anything except a meek and demure glide from door to chair impossible.

"No, it's fine Amelia, really. I don't need another dress." She pulled her gold watch out of an inside skirt pocket and glanced at it. "Didn't you say we were expected at Lottie's Ladies Club at 3pm? It's nearly that now. Let's get going."

Amelia gracefully acquiesced, and in a short time they were alighting a few blocks away at the first ladies only ten pin bowling alley in the country. It had been quietly opened nearly a decade ago by a couple of rebel women who got bored at having their fun limited to card games and dancing. They'd started it purely for their private pleasure but word had spread, and the membership now included women from fifty of New York's first families.

"Place looks busy today," Elanora commented. "Hope we don't have to wait too long for a turn."

Amelia shrugged and laughed. "Who cares? We've got plenty of time to talk and have coffee." She gathered her arm around Elanora's waist, and they progressed to the Irish doorman who welcomed them with a bow and tipping of his white top hat. "Coat check that way, ladies."

They wandered through a handsomely furnished lobby with deep brown leather couches, large framed mirrors, and potted palms in bronze urns — the image, in fact, of a wealthy gentleman's club. On one side of a mahogany counter, a sign indicated the cloakroom, and beyond it the changing rooms where they would don 'bowling costumes' they could hire for a $5 ticket.

They'd been to play bowls here on half a dozen occasions, but Elanora still found herself giggling as she looked at herself in the mirror when she'd finished dressing. In white bowling pants, a blue blouse and a black cap on her head she looked like — what — Eustace's driver?

"What are you laughing at?" Amelia's face crinkled up in puzzled lines.

"Just thinking about what William would say if he could see me now. If he thought I was undesirable before …"

"Oh, Ellie, let's go and have that coffee and talk. There's a lot that needs to be said."

Elanora's heart felt like a stone in her chest. "I'm not sure talking will do any good, Amelia. It's not going to change anything."

"Not about William's attitude perhaps. But it can change how you see it."

"You've been such a good friend to me through this, Amelia, you really have. But you've got your own things to — you know — think about."

They settled into a privately situated banquette and ordered coffee and cake.

While they waited they surveyed the hall. The banquettes where they were sitting lined the outside wall, with the bowling alleys running down the center of the room. Activity was moderately busy, but Elanora was glad to see there was no one she really needed to talk to. Once the fragrant hot brew and lemon poppy seed bread was on the table, Amelia hesitated and looked around.

"You mentioned about me having my own things to talk about … There's been a development there I need to tell you about. I know you love Connie, so please don't be mad at me."

"Honestly, Amelia, I'm not even sure how much of Connie I'll be able to see in the coming months ... I've no idea."

"Don't be silly. Aunt Coco will always want to see you. You're like a second daughter to her."

"Well, maybe. But when Eustace marries ..."

Amelia hesitated. "About that. Eustace marrying. Forgive me for commenting on something so intimate, dear Ellie, but I eavesdropped on Mother and Father last night when they came back from dinner. They were talking in their room and they didn't realize I was still awake. Their door was open. I heard everything."

Elanora's stony heart felt as if it had been engulfed in a wave of fear. She didn't know if she wanted to hear what was coming next. She struggled to find her voice and cleared her throat nervously. "Talking? What about?"

"They were shocked at William's rudeness. Absolutely shocked."

Amelia looked pale in the bowling alley gas light. "Ellie, if they ever had any idea about William and me … Well, they'd murder me. You'll never tell anyone, will you?"

Elanora shook her head. "Of course not. For your sake. Not for his. He deserves whatever's coming to him."

Amelia frowned. "I suppose … Anyway, mother said the way he embarrassed you publicly was completely uncalled for. And father said it was all because he wanted everyone — Eustace, Connie and your father — to understand that Eustace would be marrying to advance family interests, and not for any other reason.

And father said ..." she paused and grimaced. "I'm sorry Ellie, but he said your father's estate brings nothing to Mountforts. So even if you were Helen of Troy herself he wouldn't let Eustace marry you."

The fear that she had felt a few seconds before flared into red hot fury. "He 'won't let him?' Eustace is nearly twenty-four, for goodness sakes. He doesn't have to be beholden to his father for every dollar."

Amelia reached over and patted her arm. "Easy to say, Ellie. Easy to say. But look at it from his point of view. He's been born and bred to take over the family business. Father says they're positioned for huge growth in the next couple of years. New York's doubling in size every decade.

"Fortunes are being made every

month. The Mountforts can't afford to be overtaken. And William will find the best alliance he can for them.

"You know how it is … Father says any businessman worth his salary understands who you marry can be the most important decision of your career. And your father — poor sick old man that he is — he's not the alliance William is looking for."

Amelia stopped suddenly, like a runaway horse baulking at the next brush fence. "I'm sorry, Elanora. I know it must be hard to hear. But can you see it from William's point of view?" She looked around anxiously as if seeking reassurance from some unidentified source.

"Father says marriages are even being taken into consideration by the Dun credit agency when they're assessing the value of a firm — so you can't blame William for being concerned." She affected a shrug and forced a smile. "You'll probably be married long before Eustace is anyway, so I'm sure it will all work out."

Elanora felt the hot rush of tears; her throat was so choked she could barely croak out a response. "I had no idea … I hadn't thought …" She steeled herself to stay calm. To not break down. She took a deep shuddering breath. "Anyway, enough about me. I'm glad you told me, Amelia. I really am. But what about you? You mentioned a 'development'?"

Amelia's cheeks flushed bright pink. "Yes, well … William has said he will send me to Paris for the summer. Like on a full art scholarship. He's going to be discussing it with my parents later this week. Says I'll be able to leave in the

New Year, long before … you know … anything shows." She blushed bright pink.

"He has someone I can stay with there — a mademoiselle with a respectable private hotel for young women. And I can study at art school for a few months and then come home when it's all over. He says he will come and visit me while I'm there."

Elanora's mouth dropped open. She stared at Amelia in disbelief.

"What? What's wrong?" Amelia's face scrunched up with uncertainty. "Have I said something?"

Have I said something? The words echoed in Elanora's head like buzzing bees. She grabbed her forehead between the fingers of her right hand and pressed the temples hard, as if hoping the exerted pressure would clear her mind.

She wasn't sure what stunned her the most about what Amelia had just told her. William Mountfort's hypocrisy at touting his son's marriage prospects while ruining the young daughter of one of his senior business partners.

Or Amelia's blithe acceptance that she would just pop out a baby, presumably leave it behind to be fostered out somewhere in France and then return home as if nothing had happened.

"Um. Amelia, I hope it all works out for you. I really do. It all seems … Well, it seems a bit far-fetched to me to be honest. Do you really think you will be able to keep this all a secret from your parents forever? And what about when you meet someone you want to marry? What then?"

Amelia's pretty mouth formed into a pout. "I know it must be hard for you,

Ellie. I mean things working out for me, and not for you."

She stood, as if she'd just remembered they were there to play bowls.

"Besides, I have met someone I want to marry." She shrugged, as if the next statement was inconsequential. "It's a pity he's already got a wife, but William says everything will work out if I'm patient."

Seven

Elanora gazed blindly out of the carriage that was taking her and Amelia home from Lottie's, her head so full of Amelia's chatter she was barely aware of her surroundings. Her father had lost his will to live since her mother's death. She knew that.

But she'd never considered his illness would harm her marriage prospects. He was comfortably off, a former solicitor who no longer practised his craft but still — she had thought — held a place of respect in New York's business circles.

She'd taken her family's place in the upper echelons of New York's commercial and professional life for granted. They rented a pew in Trinity church. She'd gone to the right private school, attended the favored dancing classes.

She knew what cutlery to use, understood the admonition for a woman to be modest at all times — everything in her upbringing prepared her to expect she'd take her place at the top table. To hear her father dismissed in the way Amelia had, admittedly based on her parent's hearsay, shocked her.

The carriage came to a sudden jolt in the Broadway traffic, and she realized with a start that they were heading downtown towards Trinity and the wharves, not uptown towards their homes closer to Fifth Avenue. She turned to Amelia in alarm.

"Where are we going? I thought you said we were going home?"

"Oh, we are, but father asked if we could go via the office and pick him up on our way. He said he'd be finishing about the time we were planning to leave, and as we've got his carriage ..."

At the mention of Amelia's father, Elanora felt nauseous. The last thing she wanted was to share a ride home with a man who'd so unflinchingly dissected what a poor prospect she was as a rising merchant's wife.

"But I need to get home. Father will start worrying."

The tight band across her forehead made her frown. "Really, Amelia. I'm not feeling well."

"We can't turn back now. We're nearly there."

Sure enough, they were rounding the square closest to Mountfort's offices — Mountfort and Wollander she didn't doubt soon — and fleetingly wondered if Wollander had a daughter William was lining up for Eustace.

She clenched her hands in her lap and fought to appear nonchalant as their ride drew to a halt outside.

"I'll stay here," Elanora said. "No need for me to come inside."

"Sure. I'll only be a minute."

Amelia's eyes had a bright anticipatory gleam. The girl was head over heels in love, Elanora saw with a lurching heart. Poor Aunt Coco. Did she have any idea? Did she care?

A tap at the window startled her out of more day dreaming. Eustace stood outside, alert and eager. "Elanora! Amelia said you were outside! Can I have a word?"

She was shaking her head before he'd completed his sentence. "No, Eustace.

I'm not feeling well. I've got a funny tummy. Not now."

He opened the door anyway and leaned in. "Dear Elanora, I've wanted to see you so much. After that dreadful scene with Father ... I'm so sorry ..."

He sucked in his cheeks and his eyes darted past her. She'd never seen him so ill at ease.

"It was awful, Eustace. It really was, I can't pretend otherwise. But this isn't the time or place."

"Why not? I want you to know ..." He gave her a longing look. "It doesn't change anything, Ellie. You know, about the way I feel ..."

The words she'd secretly been hoping to hear. He'd said them.

But instead of the weight on her heart lightening, instead of the great wave of sadness rolling away, she felt a strange blocked sensation in her ears, as if she'd gone deaf.

The man leaning adoringly over her was nearly twenty-four years old, as she kept reminding herself. He should be a man capable of making his own decisions, of raising his own family. And he was lolling against the doorway spouting nonsense. She licked her lips and waited for the funny silence in her head to disappear, while he gazed at her expectantly. And suddenly her head cleared and she was furious.

"Perhaps you feel the same way, Eustace," she said with a waspish tone. "But what about your father? That paragon of moral rectitude and politesse?" Have *his* feelings changed?"

Eustace took a step back, his jaw slack.

"Oh, come on old girl, what's got into

you? That's not like you ..."

"So has your father explained to his son and heir that the Travers blood line isn't good enough? How a sick old invalid isn't going to be of any benefit to the firm?"

A guilty, shamed expression skittered across his face, and she knew William had said something exactly like that.

"I can't believe you would go so far as to ... as to ..." her voice faltered, and a wave of dizziness washed over her. "Well, as far as giving me that ring the other night. When you knew he will never allow it." She said the words quietly, emphatically, trying to finally grasp the certainty of her disaster and not let go.

"He will never allow it."

She looked him straight in the eye. "Why did you do that?"

He stood in shamed silence, his mouth open, lost for words. She thrust up from her seat, stepped through the doorway and pushed past him into the busy late afternoon street. A curse on all the etiquette books that stipulated a lady was never to push past a gentleman.

"Elanora, you can't … Where are you going?"

"As far away from you as I can Eustace. It doesn't matter to me where that is, just a very long way away."

She plunged blindly onto Broadway, grateful to have her misery engulfed in the bright energy of the surging crowds of Christmas shoppers which had become such a thing over the past few years.

Stores stayed open till midnight on the days leading up to Christmas, and the pavements were crowded with visitors, some shopping for toys, fruit, and baubles and treasures of all kinds, others content to window shop the gorgeous succession of storefronts piled high with tempting merchandise.

She followed some boys who were busking Christmas carols with a flute and guitar, collecting dimes from cheery passers-by. They led her into a magical street lined with lit Christmas trees. She was wondering if she should buy one and take it home, and then as quickly realized there was no one at home except her who would appreciate it.

She wandered listlessly, basking in the happiness of those around her, barely aware of her progress until she found herself on a quiet back street. She paused and looked around, an uncomfortable sensation of someone at her back bringing her to sudden alertness. Ten yards or so back up the street a man with lank shoulder length hair loitered, his shifty eyes refusing to make eye contact.

She felt a shiver of discomfort and wheeled around to cross the street and move away from him. But when she glanced back, he was shadowing her progress, hanging back in the shadows but purposefully tailing her.

She castigated herself for her carelessness. There was no one else around, nowhere she could escape, and she was well off the routes where the hack cabs picked up random fares. Most of the premises in this neighborhood faced the street with block fences and locked gates.

She surged on, for the first time feeling a rising panic inside. She was being driven further and further away from the busy thoroughfare, and deeper and deeper into a dangerous unknown.

Then she saw it, up ahead, the glass front of a building that opened onto the street, some sort of merchant's premises or artist's studio?

She could hear her stalker's footsteps closing in; she glanced around wildly and saw he was coming up fast behind her. He was cross-eyed, leering at her through blackened teeth, reaching out an arm to grab her elbow.

In one quick move she got her hand to the one door she'd passed that opened to the street. An overhead bell jangled as she stumbled into a cavernous low-lit room and stood there, waiting for her heart to stop racing and her eyes to adjust to the reduced light.

Along the walls black and white portraits hung, each artfully highlighted, and with a rush of relief she realized she'd chanced upon one of the many daguerreotype studios that had opened on and off Broadway — she'd heard fifteen or more of them in this area alone.

The portraits on the walls were overwhelming in their intense simplicity, and the panicky fear she'd felt moments ago lifted like a weight from across her shoulders as she gazed toward them. The big room was silent, as if wrapped in a blanket of serenity and protection. She hastily glanced to where she'd come in. The door was firmly shut, and no one had followed her.

With a deep sigh of gratitude, she tiptoed across the room and sank onto a leather covered ottoman, clearly placed there for visitors to sit and contemplate the images. She felt as if she'd arrived in a safe harbor, but wasn't sure if she was permitted to dock. It was like slipping past St Peter to gain entry to heaven. For now, she was just glad to be free of the lout tailing her.

Through a doorway at the back, the dimness was pierced by sparkling pin points of light. A myriad of slender candles, fixed with an array of other twirling red, yellow, blue decorations shone out from the branches of a fresh smelling Christmas tree. The clean pine fragrance reached across the space and dispelled the final threads of jittery panic that had enveloped her.

Her ragged breathing slowed back to normal, and a wave of calm wellbeing flooded in. This was her world. She recognized some of these people — well known burghers and politicians. She thought she even spotted a former US President among them.

She allowed herself to slump with relief into the soft padded leather. She was safe. She was strong. She was unhurt. And her philandering once-upon-a-time father-in-law was not going to destroy her.

Rafael Castellanos y Ordonez was putting the finishing touches to a photographic plate in the back room of the Philip Haas Gallery when he heard the street door jangle its warning alert.

The gallery space at the front was elegantly fitted out, but out the back was much more utilitarian. Here were the operating rooms where young boys cleaned and buffed the metal plates, where the cameras were set up, and where trained technicians developed, fixed and framed the images.

Funny. They weren't expecting their

visitors to start arriving for another half hour. His German colleague Haas was a celebrated daguerreotypist with a flair for sales, and tonight they were holding a Christmas reception for key clients and enthusiasts with all the festive trimmings from Haas's homeland.

There'd be mulled wine, rum balls and roasted chestnuts, musical entertainment and gifts for the children. And, of course, an opportunity for potential customers to admire the latest work and commission portraits of themselves or their loved ones. They had a big night planned — but it wasn't due to begin for another hour.

He quickly finished the delicate print he was working on and wiped his hands on a towel before ducking his head through the doorway into the main gallery. A young woman rested on one of the gallery ottomans, deeply contemplative, gazing up at the portrait of John Quincy Adams, the sixth president of the United States.

He stepped into the room, and she started at the sound of his boot hitting the floor. "Can I be of assistance, madam?"

She rose, half in alarm, as if she'd been caught eavesdropping or shoplifting.

"No … no, I'm absolutely fine, thank you. Couldn't be better really." She laughed in a low musical rush, enjoying, it seemed, a private joke, because he couldn't see anything amusing.

"I was Christmas window shopping and I got waylaid." Her face clouded over. "And then I got followed by a worrisome vagrant. Actually, I was semi-lost. And I found safe harbor." She smiled.

He stepped across the room, his hand outstretched, to greet her formally.

"Rafael Castellanos y Ordonez at your service Miss …"

He took her hand in his and felt the lingering iciness.

"Elanora Travers," she said. "My father was a lawyer with one of the local import houses down on the wharves until he was invalided."

"I see. So a born and bred New Yorker?"

"That's right. And this gallery? Is it your gallery?"

"Oh no, no, I've only recently arrived in New York. Philip Haas is a celebrated photographer. One of the pioneers in fact. We met in Paris. We were both fascinated by the new daguerreotype process and had gone there to learn more. You knew it started there?"

She hunched her shoulders forward in a wistful shrug. "I guess … I haven't had much opportunity to learn about it. But these portraits … They are wonderful. You feel as if the soul is bared … And what it shows sometimes isn't what the sitter might have been expecting." She gave another light, tuneful laugh. "I imagine appearances don't always deceive, at least when Mr Haas is at work. I presume this is his work — or is it yours?"

"Oh no, all his. As I say, I'm just getting started."

She stepped toward him and offered him her arm. "So you are also a daguerreotypist, Mr Castellanos? Why don't you show me around the exhibits, and explain the finer points of your art to me."

He accepted the gesture of friendship

with a smile. "Delighted, I'm sure. We have a few minutes before our guests arrive for our Christmas show. And if you don't have to be somewhere else, I'm sure Philip would be delighted to have you stay for that as well."

She inclined her head gracefully toward him. "My turn to be delighted, I'm sure. My fairy godmother has given me permission to stay out tonight. After everything that's happened today, it feels like it was meant to be."

Eight

The trees in Astor House's central courtyard were a glittering spectacle of Christmas lights. The air hummed with sweet music and the pop of champagne corks as Elanora made her way through the festive throng. Everyone who was anyone attended Sarah and John Jacob Astor's Christmas party, and elegantly dressed women flocked together like a myriad of brightly colored parrots in their multi-hued full-skirted gowns.

As she progressed forward slowly, she nodded and bowed to numerous acquaintances — girls from school in bright pink and turquoise; her mother's generation in more sober plum and olive green.

No one watching her would have guessed that her heart skittered in her chest as she walked alongside her father's chair. Henry Travers' chair was tonight being managed by Boston Dowd, the muscular gray-haired manservant her father employed to attend to all his physical needs.

Tonight she had to pull off one of the best performances of her life, to appear as if she had not a care in the world. She ignored her unruly heart, beating hot and erratic. The brainless organ was anticipating the meeting with Eustace — the first time they would have been together since their heated confrontation two days before. Her heart was reacting, and nothing her head told her made any difference.

She didn't regret walking out on him, and she still didn't believe they had a future. He'd made no attempt to call on her in the days since, and for that she was strangely grateful.

She allowed herself a brief smile as she thought back to the serendipity of that night — her frantic need to get away from the man stalking her, and her remarkable meeting with Rafael Castellanos and his friend Philip Haas.

She'd been welcomed like a patroness of the studio; Rafael had discussed the finer points of photography in a way that made her feel included in an exclusive circle.

And then Philip and his wife Mary had hosted their delightful European-style party, with gifts for everyone — coupons offering a discount on sittings and cigars for the men, pretty lockets with space for an image to be housed in the casing for the ladies, and pretty painted miniature toys for the children. There seemed to be lots of children.

What with the warmed Gluhvein — she didn't need Rafael's joking warning to go easy on the 'glow wine' — and the excited laughter of the children, she'd forgotten all her troubles. The evening's spicy cardamom and cinnamon fragrance came back to her as she recalled the moment. She thought wistfully of the time when her mother was alive and they'd shared that kind of joyful family life. It had evaporated in the years since her mother's death.

When Mr Castellanos kindly saw her to the safety of a hired hack cab to take her home, she'd found that her father had retired to bed early and Boston advised that she hadn't been missed.

She straightened her shoulders and paused mid-stride as she looked around the Astor House courtyard. Despite some serious new competition, it was still considered New York's premium hotel, and tonight it was truly living up to that claim.

The central courtyard was ringed with bowers arched with greenery and pretty lights which picked up flashes from snow crystals still evident on the ground, but the air temperature was pleasantly mild thanks to a very effective gas heating system.

No sit-down meal was planned, but an army of servants circulated with trays laden with delicacies that they offered guests in passing or deposited on round tables. Hot spiced punch in crystal tumblers, shrimps in saffron cream, smoked trout on potato pancakes, fried asparagus, smoked pheasant in puff pastry, mustard eggs, stuffed cabbage rolls, and duck liver pate. The tables were piled high.

The footman who'd been guiding Boston to the correct table bowed and left, and they began the customary greetings. William was talking to an older man she didn't recognize and neither Eustace nor Amelia were in evidence. Mingling no doubt.

Aunt Coco sat quietly on a bench seat backed into the green archway looking pale and drawn. Elanora felt a jolt of alarm. Eustace's mother looked ill. Seriously ill. She quietly made her way to her side and sank down beside her.

"Dear Aunt, so lovely to see you. I hope you are feeling well this evening? Are you keeping warm?"

"I am perfectly fine, dear girl. Just a little tired. Comes with old age I suppose." Her tender gray eyes searched

Elanora's face. "How about you Elanora?" She reached out and placed a hand consolingly on her arm. "I can't express how bad I feel about that dreadful scene William threw the other night. I don't know what's gotten into the man."

Elanora leaned in and brushed her Aunt's cheek with her lips. She then bent in closer, right next to her ear and whispered. "Please don't mention it, dear Coco. I know it doesn't reflect your views, and I'd prefer to forget about it."

She knew Connie would not miss the tight set on her jaw as she pulled back, fighting to maintain full control of her emotions. "Things happen." She squeezed her Aunt's hand affectionately. "We can't always expect a straight road."

She sensed people around her stirring,

and she glanced up to see Amelia was back, dragging behind her none other than Rafael Castellanos.

"Elanora. Look who I've got here. The Spanish photographer who took Mrs Astor's portrait. They've set up a daguerreotype booth in the main foyer and anyone can get their picture taken for free! Let's do it Ellie. To remember the days of our youth."

Castellanos was watching her with an eagle eye, and when Amelia finished talking he made a slight bow. "Miss Travers. How very pleasant to meet you again."

Amelia's jaw dropped. "Again? When did you meet before?" She eyeballed Elanora with a mischievous glint. "Secret assignations, hey? You are a dark horse."

Elanora felt her cheeks flush. "Nothing

like that, Amelia. That night when I made my own way home from your father's office, I went via Mr Philip Haas's studio and was lucky enough to be invited to a delightful Christmas celebration there — all done in the German tradition, wasn't it, Mr Castellanos?"

His deep black eyes bored into her, and then a smile lit his face. "Yes indeed, in the German tradition. Philip is a stickler for it, true American soul though he is."

Amelia clasped at Elanora's arm. "Never mind all that. Let's go now and have our image taken. You never know if we'll get another opportunity." She blushed and Elanora guessed she was anticipating her still-secret planned trip to Paris.

Elanora glanced over to Aunt Coco. "Is

that OK, Coco? We won't leave you for long"

"Off you go. Have some fun. It's Christmas!"

As they made their way to the photographic booth, shepherded courteously by Castellanos, Elanora became aware of the Spaniard's already substantial social networks. Every few steps stylish woman or their teenaged daughters smiled, nodded greetings, gave a little wave or plain simpered at him.

He was quite a favorite with the first ladies of New York. She wondered how she'd missed out on that piece of intelligence and realized she'd not really had time for any man except Eustace for months now.

A jabbing jaw pain brought her up short; she was grinding her teeth and clenching her fists as if gearing herself up to fight. Her face was hot again. She couldn't be jealous, could she? She hardly knew the man. Then she did something she was getting good at. She faced the truth fair and square.

She didn't like the approving female attention Rafael Castellanos was effortlessly harvesting. The man just had to stalk that prowling lion-like walk and fix them with those cool detached eyes and they fell over themselves to win his undivided attention. He seemed oblivious to it, but it annoyed her anyway. For goodness sakes, what was wrong with her?

"You didn't tell me you were running away when we met the other night." With the photo session over, Amelia had disappeared off with William and Eustace to meet mutual friends.

She'd held back, and Rafael, sensing her reluctance, had offered to escort her back to Aunt Coco's side. But no sooner had the others left, than he'd issued his challenge, his voice low and confidential, like he was sharing a secret with her.

The surge of pleasure that coursed through her at the intimacy of the moment was doused in the next second by the recognition that she was as bad as all the rest of the twittering females, craving his individual attention. She tried to distance herself from her feelings.

"Running away? I don't know what you mean. I told you about the bothersome man who followed me."

"Yes, but you didn't tell me you were wandering the streets because you'd had a lover's quarrel."

She could feel her face flushing red,

and she stammered as she answered. "A quarrel? What gives you that impression?"

"Come on, Miss Elanora. When you're operating in a second — or third — language as I am, you get a lot better at observing the silent communication. The language which doesn't require words."

She always wondered later if this was the moment she fell in love with Rafael — the moment when he called her out on her play acting.

Her heart felt like it had plummeted to her boots as she regarded him in silence, following the intelligent, thoughtful flickering across his face, the cool assessment in his eyes, the wolfish twitch of his lips. With a shock she understood; with this man, she didn't need to use words. He was already a master at reading his subject's silences.

He didn't look away, and as they locked eyes she felt stripped of all the lies, the pretensions, she was still holding onto. He addressed her in a low, considered tone.

"I'd very much like to do a portrait of you — free of charge of course. You have such a strong individual face — beautiful it goes without saying — but so much more is revealed there. Let me do this and any debt you owe me for 'rescuing' you the other night is forgiven."

He suddenly dropped the intense gaze and gave her a predacious grin. "Have we got a deal? You'll be helping me immensely to achieve recognition as the daguerreotypist to New York's 'top fifty' if you do.

"I've been fortunate enough to photograph Sarah Astor, yes. But forgive me for saying, she's no oil painting. I'm confident the younger set will fall over themselves to be photographed once they see what I've done with you."

He dropped his eyes from her face, and when he glanced back up, his mood had changed to one that was playful, even flirtatious. "The worst photographer in the world couldn't make you look bad, and I'm one of the best."

Nine

They slipped through Trinity Church's heavy bronze doors into their rented pew — Number 95 — just ahead of the crocodile of white and gold gowned clergy and choir boys lining up for Christmas Eve Midnight Mass. Elanora drew aside the fur-trimmed hood of the mantle that protected her head and shoulders from the lightly falling snowflakes. She was glad for its satin quilted lining because the church was as cold inside as it was in the yard outside.

They always seemed to be late these days. What with her father's fragile health and the delays with carriages negotiating the icy crowded streets, transporting him around town was increasingly difficult. She wondered how much longer he'd be able to go out and about — and what it would do to his spirits to be stuck at home.

Boston Dowd leaned across and said in a hoarse whisper. "He's happily settled." The organ sounded the trumpet-like signal that the officiants were about to start processing, and she replied with a quick smile.

The doughty assistant had once again done the heavy lifting to get Henry's chair aligned at the end of the row, well out of the way of incense-swinging thurifer who was even now leading the solemn file of priests and musicians to Trinity's stained-glass jewel of a Gothic altar.

She settled into the wooden pew and took in the familiar panorama: the back-head view of some of the people she knew best in the world, framed by the awe-inspiring pointed Gothic arch at the end of the chancel, its three dazzling layers of glass — Jesus at the center, lined either side by the disciples and saints — Peter, Matthew, Mark, Luke and the apostle Paul — displayed for all to see.

She resisted the way her heart lurched at the sight of the Mountfort pew, a dozen rows in front. William sat half a shoulder taller than Eustace, but there was no sign of Aunt Coco. She felt a pang of concern. Her aunt had not looked well the other night, and she hadn't been able to call in to see her since. She hoped she was waylaid by something trivial.

On the opposite side of the aisle, halfway between where she sat and the

Mountforts, she sought out Amelia and her parents, the three huddled together, the epitome of the happy burgher family. Will and Adelaide flanked their daughter, who radiated beauty in an emerald green dress with a pagoda sleeve. She recognized it as one she often wore, with a nipped bodice that highlighted her tiny waist.

The procession was well past her now; the incense carrier and the boy with an incense box had passed by, followed by the crucifer with a large gold cross held like a battle standard, and then two acolytes carrying lighted candles. And then all the rest — clergy and singers. The whole train paused at a model crib with a baby in it set up at the end of the nave, and the rector William Berrian stepped up to bless the baby Jesus.

Elanora's eyes flicked to Amelia, who

was looking blissfully secure in her emerald green. A shiver ran through her. How she managed to appear so unconcerned, when she was carrying such a ruinous secret — Elanora's heart chilled at the thought. What if the indiscretion she'd permitted with Eustace had left her in the same condition? She felt sick in her stomach, and immediately worried that thinking it might make it so.

They'd just have to marry if that happened. She chewed her lip as the service got under way, the words from the pulpit washing over her as a faint background chorus as she reflected on her situation. If the impossible, the dreadful, the unlikely happened and she was carrying Eustace's child, she'd have to tell him. They'd have to marry.

A week ago, that thought would have sent her into ecstasy. Now it was accompanied by a dull ache across the back of her neck. She'd be forever yoked not just to Eustace, but to his father, carrying the knowledge like an incubus her whole life that she was not good enough, that she'd kept Eustace from a union that would advance the family's fortunes so much better than she could.

Bile rose in her throat even as she contemplated the prospect. And what of Eustace? Did he see things the same way as his father, really? What if she told him about Amelia, told him he should be expecting a half-brother or a half-sister in seven or eight months' time?

Would he be shocked at his father's duplicity? A man concerned about fostering an illustrious public face while he was abusing Will and Adelaide's trust? If she told Eustace about William's secret life, would it change anything?

She was startled back into the present
by the pealing of a pretty musical bell —
not the big clappers in the bell tower, but
a musical hand bell rung by one of the
servers before the choir led the
congregation in the Sanctus. "Holy, Holy,
Holy Lord … God of Power and Might …
Hosanna in the Highest."

As she stood to join in the chorus, she
caught Amelia's eye. Her friend beamed
and looked at her intently, communicating
silently across heads bowed over prayer
books. *Catch you later …*

She looked incandescent, eyes
sparkling, teeth pearly white and even in
a rosebud pink mouth. So what was up
now? And poor Aunt Coco. Elanora
wasn't at all sure she wanted to know.

"Elanora, you've got to understand!"

The gold flecked brown eyes that had

always held mystery for him gazed back, uncomprehending. She touched the base of her throat, as if fumbling for a locket or necklace, coming up with empty fingers.

Eustace took her hands gently in his and held them as he gazed down at her. "Please! Listen to me. I love you! I want to marry you!"

Her lips pressed together in a flat, tight line.

"Eustace, I'm sure you believe what you are saying."

Her voice had taken on the measured, reasoning tone of an adult talking to someone younger.

"But it doesn't change anything. Your father is opposed to us. Don't you understand that? And he's not going to change his mind." She glanced away despairingly. "He's decided he wants a merchant house heiress to further the Mountfort empire. And I don't fit the requirements." Her voice caught in her throat and her eyes dropped to the floor.

When she looked back up at him her face was set like stone. "I. Don't. Meet. His requirements."

They were sitting in the deserted Trinity nave, partially hidden by a choir screen, while the rest of the Christmas Eve congregation chattered and laughed and sipped sherry and ate fruit mince tarts in the downstairs supper room. He'd been desperate to get her to one side and explain the situation, but the conversation was not going as he'd anticipated.

"Mother will sort it out, sweetheart. She always does. Don't you worry. She always does."

When he'd uttered such assurances to

himself in the past he'd felt warm and full. Tonight, he acknowledged, he was cold and empty inside.

His mother had taken to her bed after the Astor House party. Perhaps she'd got a chill from being too long sitting around on that stone bench.

She'd complained of sharp pains in her lower back, and then she'd developed a fierce fever, which he still couldn't bring himself to mention to Elanora. He was hoping it would leave as quickly as it had come on, with no lasting harm.

One thing was for sure, in her current state, Connie wasn't capable of persuading anyone of anything. She was using every ounce of her considerable reserves to hold onto life.

Elanora's eyes held the question he didn't want to answer.

"Aunt Coco? How is she? And why isn't she here tonight? She's OK, isn't she?"

"Yes, yes, just a bit under the weather after the Astor House do. Think she stayed out too late and got a bit of a chill."

She nodded with a distracted air, as if her mind was already somewhere else, and snuggled into the mantle across her shoulders.

"Eustace, can't you see that your father doesn't listen to Connie like he used to anyway? He's changed." She faltered and looked away again. He sensed there was something else she wanted to say.

"What? What is it?"

"Your father. William ... Eustace, he's got secrets. You'd be shocked to know ..." She turned suddenly, and her eyes locked to his, a fierce set to her jaw. "I didn't want to know, truly. I was an unwilling confidante. But he's … he's being unfaithful to Connie."

Eustace felt the uncertainty that had gripped him at her sudden urgency melt away. "Oh Elanora, sweetheart." He laughed quietly. "It's what men of our …" He quickly corrected himself. "His station do. You know that, don't you? It's not uncommon to go to the pleasure houses. Wives don't always have to be available. Some might even prefer it that way …"

He stopped as the color drained from her face. "Not that I'd consider such a thing myself. Never. It's not like that … But you can't be too naive about the world's ways if you're getting married." He patted her hand affectionately.

She drew back from him with a jolt. "No, Eustace, you don't understand. I

117

don't mean that way. I mean he's taking advantage of a young girl from our own group. And she's with child."

He gave an involuntary gasp and shook his head. "Who told you that? It's lies ... It must be." A red tide had risen in front of his eyes, and he was squinting, rubbing his eye sockets, trying to make the semi-blindness go away.

"No. I can't believe it. It's like that bishop a few years back — what was his name — Oderling or something? He was accused of licentiousness by those women — and it all turned out to be lies to stop him introducing high church stuff. None of our crowd believed them. I bet this is the same sort of thing. Something an enemy has dragged up. It must be."

Tears were rolling down Elanora's cheeks, as she shook her head, sobbing. "It isn't like that Eustace. Not at all. And

I wouldn't be surprised if he wants to broker a good marriage for you before word gets out and ruins your family's reputation."

He was on his feet in a flash, stepping back from her, their hands no longer within touching distance. His ears roared.

"Elanora, how could you? I never thought it of you. Never."

"Never thought what?"

"That you'd repeat such lies to try and get what you want. How many other people have you gossiped about this to?" He shook his head admonishingly. "You're not a kid any more, Elanora. Don't you realize what harm you're doing by repeating such tales?"

She broke down into racking sobs. "They are not tales, Eustace. I'm very sorry, but they are not stories."

He shook his head. "You didn't need

to do it, Elanora. I would have married you anyway. But being willing to believe such lies about the man who would be your father-in-law … How could you?"

He turned to go, suddenly unwilling to be near her. A final thought struck him as he wheeled on his heel to stride out. "And for goodness sakes, don't go spouting any of this nonsense to my mother. In her current state of health, she might not survive it."

Ten

"So sorry to have missed you yesterday, Elanora. I do hope you are feeling better today." Amelia smiled sympathetically and presented the cloth-covered basket she carried with a flourish.

"Cook sent over some Boxing Day goodies for you and your father. She always was so fond of old Henry. She's packed some of the things she knows he likes — like marzipan, and rum balls."

"That's so kind of you."

They were sitting in front of a glowing fire in the drawing room, Elanora in a simple day dress, hugging her stoneware hot water bottle to her chest for comfort. Christmas Day 1847 had been the quietest and loneliest of her twenty-one years. Neither she nor her father felt well enough to go out when they woke the morning after the Trinity Mass, and they'd sent their apologies to the Taylor household where they'd been expected for a quiet family lunch.

Henry was simply exhausted after his late night, and Elanora, truth be told, did not have the strength to face anyone after her cataclysmic rupture with Eustace. She wanted nothing but to curl up and hide away, nursing her pain.

She couldn't believe he'd impute selfish motives to her attempt to confide in him. He actually believed she would cook up false charges against his father in a spiteful attempt to force him to marry her? She felt sick in her stomach at the thought.

Did he really think he was that

desirable, and she was that desperate? She felt hot every time she recalled the way the conversation had barrelled out of control.

"Are you OK, Elanora? You don't seem yourself."

Amelia smiled at her with her wide, artless blue eyes. It must be wonderful to see the world in such simple dimensions. Elanora felt mean even thinking it, but really. Either Amelia was completely without a smidgeon of soul or she was incapable of seeing beyond her own self-interest. The discomfort her actions caused others just did not seem to register.

"I'm fine, Amelia, just fine, thank you. I think I just caught a little chill on Christmas Eve. I had my mantle on, but maybe I got too damp getting into the church in the snowfall." She smiled weakly.

"I hope you haven't got the same thing Eustace's mother has. Apparently she isn't at all well. She didn't get up for Christmas lunch either, I'm told. She stayed in bed."

Elanora's heart clenched. She'd been so upset she hadn't wanted to face Connie. She remembered Eustace's throw-away remark. At the time she'd put it down to his fury at having his father's reputation questioned.

As if there were any way she'd tell her beloved Coco about his horrid deceit and cause further family damage. She shook her head to make the thought go away.

"I'm sorry to hear that. I'll have to call over there sometime soon to see her."

"Oh, Eustace says she's not receiving any visitors at present. Just taking things quietly."

"Oh, alright then, fine. I'll wait till she's feeling better."

The fire popped and a spark hit the wire guard. There was an uncomfortable prolonged silence, and then Elanora felt obligated to ask: "Everything going well with you? Are you still planning to go to Paris in the New Year?"

Amelia's face lit up. "Oh, William has been so wonderful! He's got Mother and Father's approval for the whole adventure. He's just been a marvel at getting it all organized. I'm due to leave later in the month. The sixteenth I think."

"Oh, that's just wonderful Amelia. I am so happy for you." She summoned herself to rise to the occasion and share her friend's pleasure.

A shadow of doubt crossed Amelia's face, like a dark cloud racing with the wind. It was there for a moment and then it was gone. "Do you think so? It's going to be alright, isn't it?"

The anxious high note in her voice betrayed her uncertainty. "Sounds like William is ready to ensure it. You're a lucky girl."

The doorbell chimed and they both started.

"More visitors, by the sound." Amelia smiled. "I'd better get going anyway. I just wanted to bring over the treats and make sure you were alright."

She rose to go, and Boston bustled in. "A visitor for you Miss Elanora. A gentleman by the name of Castellanos."

Amelia gave an excited little squeal. "Well, Elanora, that's a coup! I had no idea you were entertaining the Spanish photographer. He's a bit of a Don Juan, isn't he? What will Eustace say?" Her eyes sparkled with mischief. "Oh, don't worry. I won't tell him."

"It's not like that, Amelia. He's interested in doing some daguerreotypes, that's all, but nothing's come of it so far."

"Oh, I'm sure." The dimples either side of Amelia's mouth showed through her smile. "I'll leave you two to it then."

Santo Dios! The love affair must be going worse even than the last time I saw her, at the Astor House party.

The American girl was pale, her expression strained. Not so happy about the things she'd just been talking about with her friend either, the one he'd just seen leaving.

Rafael followed the house manager or butler — with his powerful shoulders hunched forward he walked like a boxer, but his long gray locks and wire-rimmed spectacles gave him the mild look of a bank clerk. Rafael paused in the doorway of the warm drawing room as he was announced.

Elanora Travers had half risen from her armchair to greet him. She was dressed in a simple V-neck day dress of pale green stripes topped with a floaty shawl in green and gold tied at the neck with a bright satin ribbon. He stopped and took in the sight. Her translucent beauty shone through despite her subdued mood.

"Miss Travers, I am sorry to call without an appointment, but I was uncertain of how to reach you any other way. Forgive me if this is not a good time." He swept his arm across his body and bowed low. "I am happy to offer any service I can on this chilly day."

She smiled at the obvious gallantry and gestured to the chair abutting hers.

"Sit down, Mr Castellanos. I have been out of sorts, I admit, but you've brought fresh energy with you. Can you stay for coffee?"

"Most certainly."

Elanora looked to the boxer clerk and said, "Boston, would you be kind enough to ask Mrs O'Loughlin for coffee for two? And a little pound cake if she has it."

"I imagine you were thinking of that portrait session we discussed, is that right, Mr Castellanos? I'm afraid I am not at my best at the present. We might have to delay a week or so."

"A week, my lady? That seems excessive. Are you ill?"

"Not ill, exactly. Just out of sorts."

"I sense your mood is much subdued, Miss Travers. But I assure you if anything, the complexity of your beauty is enhanced even more by it. And yes, I was going to suggest you allow me to make an appointment for our sitting. From my point of view, it can't happen too quickly. I'm capitalizing on the economic advantage, you see. Guilty as charged."

"Guilty as charged." His finely sculpted lips twitched, and it took all of her self-control not to playfully reach over the arm of the chair he rested in and punch him.

Didn't the etiquette books say never make physical contact with a male? She'd be justified, she protested to herself. He was oh-so-gently making fun of her solemnity, of her concern for appearances.

Once again, her heart lurched at his

boldness. Rafael Castellanos y Ordonez — yes even his name was substantial — had the gift of throwing out the most unexpected conversational hooks without causing offense, and she was thrilled by it. Alongside his deep purpose, Eustace was a shadow of weak-willed predictability.

"Honestly, I beg off for today. Perhaps tomorrow?"

A tap at the door interrupted the discussion, and Mrs O'Loughlin appeared with the coffee and pound cake. When they'd settled back, he took a few sips of his coffee and put the cup down with a decisive flick of the wrist.

"Tomorrow then. Can I arrange for a horse coach to fetch you at midday?"

She nodded. "I'll have to speak to my father, but that should be fine. We won't need the horse coach I don't think —

Father has a carriage and Boston can drive me. Father would probably prefer that."

"Come to Philip's gallery. We've got it set up to get the best light. I'll expect you sometime before 1 pm. We have a woman photographer who could be present if that would help you feel more settled."

She nodded. "I'd like that. I did so love being there the other night. And having seen what Philip achieved with his portraits, I'll be curious to see how mine turns out."

He looked her in the face, his eyes sparkling.

"It will be the talk of the town, I promise. For all the best reasons."

She couldn't hide the slight recoil his words prompted. "Oh, I don't want to be the talk of the town. For any reason."

His searching dark eyes raked her.

"Why not? You are one of the most beautiful women in New York. Why not be proud of that?"

She shrugged. "I don't welcome the attention. My father isn't well …" Her voice petered out, and she was at a loss for what to say next.

I've been shamed in love and I just want to disappear through the cracks? I'm about to be revealed as a 'fallen woman' with no protector?

"It just doesn't seem wise to be too prominent." Even to her own ears she sounded feeble.

They sat in silence for a few minutes, and then she pushed the plate of pound cake to him with a bright smile. "Do have another piece, Mr Castellanos."

He ignored the cake and gazed deep into her eyes.

"Remember what I said the other

night about the silence that speaks louder than words? Forgive me my forthrightness, Miss Travers, but I must say it. Any man who lets you slip through his fingers is a fool who deserves to spend the rest of his life in regret. And if there is any such person in your world, sweet Elanora, that is exactly where he will end his days."

She stared at him, her heart in her mouth, tears pricking at the back of her eyes, and fought to retain her composure. Finally, she cleared her throat and took a deep breath, but before she could speak he reached out and gently touched her arm.

"Please. Words are not necessary. I will let myself out. I will expect you between noon and one tomorrow. And wear something simple and understated. Your magnificent presence is all I will need."

Eleven

"I have to go, Elanora. I have no other choice."

Eustace's throat choked up. "Father says there's a brigantine sailing the day after tomorrow and I am to be on it."

He put his arms around her and drew her to his shoulder; bent down and whispered in her ear, "But please, dear Elanora. Please wait for me. Give me a chance to satisfy my father's demands and then return for you. I will work it out somehow."

She was stiff and unresponsive in his arms, and he stepped back and glanced around uncomfortably, as if expecting to see her father.

"Sorry. I didn't mean ..."

"It's alright. I just don't want Father to come upon us." She gave a wry shrug. "It wouldn't look good, you know. His pure daughter in a young man's arms." She gave a bitter laugh.

They were seated in the Travers' family drawing room with the door to the hallway ajar, so as to reassure Boston — and by association her father — that they were conducting normal social chit chat. It was the day before New Year's Eve, and the temperatures were still raw out, but the room was warm from the fire that glowed in the metal grate.

"Eustace ..." She glanced uncertainty towards the door and lowered her voice to a whisper. "Eustace, what if I'm in the family way." She blushed. "You know ... from the other night."

A tight cramping sensation gripped his

lower regions. "You couldn't be." His heart was racing at double speed. And then a thought dawned, like an early sunrise, calming him. "Oh, Elanora, you haven't been talking to that female — whoever she was — the one who made all those dreadful allegations about my father? She hasn't been filling your head with more nonsense, has she?"

Elanora's face faded to chalk, and the lines across her forehead deepened into dark shadows. She began shaking her head in frantic denial. "No, Eustace, no of course not."

"Because you know, it's just not possible. Not just one time and … Well, I was careful — you don't need to know the details, but I was careful. There's no way that could happen."

Elanora squeezed her eyes tightly closed and then opened them again. "It's just — well, you'd given me the ring, and I thought we were going to be married, so it all felt right. But now it's different. If you're not even here, who can I turn to? I'm just saying ..." She grabbed for his hand. "I'm frightened, Eustace. What if I am and you aren't here?"

His chest tightened. He had never seen Elanora like this, insecure and needy, and he realized with a shock he didn't like it.

"It won't happen, Elanora. I've told you."

His voice had a tart note he hadn't intended, and she pulled back as if he'd slapped her.

He cleared his throat and adjusted his tone to something more conciliatory and reassuring. "Look, if disaster did strike, I suppose I'd have to go to my father and explain. Ask for his permission to marry you. He wouldn't like it but —"

He glanced up and just had time to brace himself. Elanora pushed him hard in the chest with both hands. He staggered back until the backs of his legs hit the edge of the sofa and he could steady himself. "What? What was that for?"

"If you don't know what that was for then you're a bigger fool than I thought you were." Her eyes were blazing as she stood, hands on hips, glaring.

Footsteps sounded in the hall, and she dropped her hands to her sides and relaxed her posture. "Eustace, you need to go."

She turned toward the door just as her father's chair nudged into the room. Henry Travers looked like he was in his last days. One arm lay curled up and useless in his lap, the other trembled with a palsy. His head dropped on his neck, as if holding it upright was beyond his power.

"Everything alright here, young Mountfort? Not upsetting my girl, are you?"

"No sir. Of course not, sir." Eustace looked to Elanora in silent appeal. She stared stonily back.

"Eustace just popped in to say goodbye, Father. He's off to the Indies on New Year's Day."

Her voice momentarily cracked at 'Indies', but her stance was fierce, her head erect, and she wasn't giving an inch.

"He's just leaving."

Twelve

Elanora had thought she'd never see a worse day in her life that when her mother died two years before, but she'd been wrong. Today, on January 6, 1848, a worse day even than that of her mother's death had dawned. It was the day they were burying her precious Aunt Coco.

New York had woken to a dense, clammy fog on the Hudson River and bone chilling temperatures that left her numb inside and out. She'd fallen into so deep a hole in herself she was barely aware of the pallbearers carrying in the elm wood coffin with black ruffles around the lid which they placed down in front of the Trinity altar.

Beside her in the bare wood pew looped with thick black cord and white lilies sat the solid comforting presence of Gloria Patience Grayson — her Aunt Glory — her mother's sister and an old friend of Connie's.

Her aunt slipped her gloved hand into hers and gave it a gentle squeeze as the organ sounded the chords for the first hymn. 'Oh God Our Help in Ages Past', that anthem that had reminded generations of mourners of the brevity of life and the eternal everlastingness of God.

The simple warmth of her aunt's gesture pierced the ice encasing her heart and the tears she'd been holding back for days overflowed. She wasn't sure which was easier to handle — feeling like she had when she'd first woken, iced up and disconnected, or feeling the thaw of her heart's loss.

She dabbed at her eyes with her free hand and pressed her fingers onto Glory's wrist in grateful response.

In the last minutes of 1847, Constance Mercy Mountfort had died in her bed in her Fifth Avenue mansion from typhus — a disease of the slums — contracted, her family believed, when she was going about her charitable endeavours.

The thing that upset Elanora the most was that she had never got to say goodbye, never got to tell Aunt Coco what she meant to her. Her rift with Eustace had made it awkward for her to visit, and she had dismissed his remarks on Christmas Eve as a spiteful, throw-away line to get at her.

She hadn't realized how serious it was until it was too late. It was so like Coco not to want a fuss made, even when she was in her last days.

Apart from a brief attendance at the Mountfort home with her father to pay their respects two days after her death, she'd seen nothing of Eustace since their terrible argument before New Year's Eve. And on the day they'd visited, he'd barely been aware she was there, consumed as he was by his own grief. For that she was grateful because as far as she was concerned there was nothing left for them to say.

The round-faced rector was opining in a bored tone. "The liturgy for the dead is an Easter liturgy. It finds all its meaning in the Resurrection. Because Jesus was raised from the dead, we, too shall be raised."

Connie certainly believed that, and Elanora fervently hoped she was right.

The thought of no Connie existing anywhere in the universe, gone in a puff of smoke, was too awful to contemplate.

Bible readings, another hymn, and the bland-faced rector rose to deliver the eulogy, praising Constance Mercy Mountfort's selfless devotion to serving the less fortunate. William sustained a fit of coughing in the middle, with Eustace coming to his rescue with consoling back thumping.

She wondered what their household would be like without Connie, and then remembered Eustace wouldn't be there anyway. She supposed William would just spend a lot more time at his men's club.

Before she knew it, they were spilling outside into the churchyard, a sliver of sunlight ineffectual in lifting the fog as they followed the coffin to the graveside.

The rector intoned the committal "earth to earth, ashes to ashes, dust to dust …" And it was all over. Connie's empty shell had been consigned to the hazardously icy ground.

"Is there anyone you need to see here, Elanora?" Gloria Grayson glanced around the crowded churchyard. Despite the weather, many of New York's leading citizens had turned out to pay their respects to Aunt Coco, and to offer condolences to her husband. She turned back to Elanora with a worried look.

"If not, then I think it will be wise to just get ourselves home. It's a day to give the healthiest body pneumonia. I certainly don't think your father should be out too long." She squinted around her again.

"And what do close family remember of a funeral anyway? It's all just one heart-wrenching blur. There will be plenty of opportunities to offer condolences in coming days, don't you think?"

Elanora's insides warmed with a surge of relief. "I couldn't agree more, dear Glory. Let's find Boston and get Father home."

She glanced around for her father's wheelchair and saw Amelia weaving her way through the throngs of mourners toward her. She was wearing an elegantly cut black astrakhan lamb's wool coat and a neat pillbox hat with a half veil that gave her an air of allure. Among the other drably garbed mourners she stood out. Aunt Glory frowned. "Is that Amelia Taylor? My goodness, hasn't she grown up."

Elanora couldn't help feeling pleased by the undertone of doubt her voice carried.

Cock-a-hoop no doubt, about this

latest development. I'm guessing she's imagining herself as the new Mrs William Mountfort in no time at all.

She flattened her simple black cap with a side mourning cockade firmly down on her head as she reproved herself for her meanness.

She's just a young woman caught in awful circumstances. It's the man who's old enough to be her father who should have known better.

"Elanora, there you are. I've been looking for you."

Elanora swung towards her Aunt. "Amelia, I'm sure you've met my Aunt Glory before? My mother's sister and a girlhood friend of Aunt Coco's?"

Amelia halted and extended a dainty hand. "Delighted to meet again, Miss Grayson. Sorry it's on such a sad occasion."

"That it is," said Aunt Glory. She took hold of Elanora's arm. "I'll go and find your father and Boston. Then we should be getting home. Shall I meet you on the sidewalk outside in five minutes? Very nice to have seen you again, Miss Taylor."

Amelia paused and waited for her to move out of earshot, and then turned to Elanora in a confidential whisper.

"Elanora, I know you were very close to Eustace's mother and losing her so soon after your own — well, I just came to say I am so sorry. If there is anything I can do …"

"Amelia, that's fine." Elanora momentarily felt guilty for her earlier thoughts. "It's an awful thing, it really is. But death — well, you know what the priests say — memento mori and all that." She gazed around the snow-covered cemetery and sighed. "'Remember you must die.' It comes to us all. Sorry, I'm rambling. I can't find too much that's cheerful to say today, so best I keep quiet."

Amelia gave a small smile. "I understand, I really do." She glanced around uncertainly.

"I'm off to Paris next week, as you know, so I'm sorry I won't be here when you're feeling more cheerful again. Not for a while, anyway ..."

She hesitated and then moved in closer to Elanora's shoulder. "William says he'll come and see me in the spring. He says we can marry quietly in Paris. He seems quite pleased at the prospect of another son."

"A son?"

"Yes. Oh well, or a daughter. He says he'd prefer a son — for the business —

but he doesn't mind."

A wave of light-headedness threatened to topple her. She reached out to grab something to hold onto and grasped Amelia's shoulder. She clutched at the fashionable curly wool.

"Sorry, Amelia. Suddenly I've come over all queer. I think today's all been a bit much for me. I'd better find Aunt Glory and my father."

She let go of the coat and Amelia stepped away. "Of course, Elanora, I understand. I'll send you a postcard."

Thirteen

Rafael Castellanos alighted from the hack on Bleecker Street and tipped the driver to wait while he crossed the street to the address Elanora had given him, a two-story house with blue shuttered windows in the popular Federal Style. From his left arm hung the leather case containing the daguerreotype images of last week's photo session.

He surveyed the brick façade. On each floor, four rows of white-silled, double-hung windows faced out onto the street. An archway, which would bear summer roses, straddled the entry, underlining the sense of comfortable prosperity.

He'd made visits to many similar

houses in recent times, calling on a portrait subject to present the results of the sitting. He should have been used to it, but this time it felt different. His heart beat faster, his core tingled with a heightened awareness and expectation. Without even being aware of her charm, Elanora Travers had reached out to him in a way that few other women had.

He'd pondered over why that was in the hours he'd spent working on the images he'd taken in his studio more than a week ago. He'd felt restless at not being able to show them to her, but it had been impossible with holiday festivities and Mrs Mountfort's death.

It was so much more than her physical beauty, though that was breathtaking. It wasn't just about the way she looked. He thought briefly of that other minxy friend of hers. She was pretty enough, but she left him unmoved.

It was a much deeper sense Elanora carried, of a yearning for bedrock truth — a fearlessness to face whatever came, to not be deceived, that he found arresting. It shone out of her gold-flecked brown eyes, in the erect fluid way she carried herself.

She'd inspired him to produce some of his best work yet. The images captured her gaiety and solemnity all in one sitting. You could sense the seeker beneath the sparkle of youth.

He stepped up the tiled path and paused at the front door. Around a weighty lion head brass door knocker hung a wreath of green olive branches trimmed in black ribbon. He hoped he wasn't offending any etiquette by calling without an appointment.

"Right. Father's favorite. Charlotte Russe coming up. We need something to cheer us."

Elanora pushed back from the kitchen table and gazed across at her Aunt Glory, perched on the other side of the kitchen table, watching with her sharp but not unkind eye. In one hand Elanora held a fine willow egg whip, balanced against the edge of a heavy earthenware bowl filled with egg whites and sugar.

She sniffed the air. The mix in the bowl gave off a heavenly vanilla and lemon fragrance. Her exertions had left her feeling pleasantly warm, and locks of blond hair had escaped from their clips and hung over her forehead.

She resisted the temptation to either

push them back, or run her damp hands down the fall of the sleeveless black gilet that covered her pale blue dress three quarters of the way to her hem, the long waistcoat her concession to mourning, along with the black and white cockade pinned to her pushed up sleeve.

"Check the oven, would you Glory. We don't want it getting too hot."

She resumed vigorously whipping the egg whites and realized with a jolt that this was the happiest she'd felt since her aunt had arrived three days ago.

The icy chill outside had not broken, and Elanora did not feel fully recovered from whatever malady had weakened her over the days of Connie's funeral. Perhaps it was just the sickness of grief, but neither she nor her aunt had any interest in leaving the house, or receiving visitors.

They'd mutually decided an afternoon baking while Mrs O'Loughlin took the afternoon off to visit her family would be great fun, mimicking times in much earlier years when they'd cooked together in her aunt's house. They'd make something to please her father, whose one last pleasure in life was the occasional sweet dessert.

"Your father will enjoy a touch of elegance." Glory looked up from the embroidery frame she was quietly stitching into as she chatted. "He hasn't got too many indulgences left to him, has he? Not that he was ever one who took license."

The Charlotte Russe was lavish and luscious, and just what they needed to banish the gloom that had descended with Connie's death.

An elegant and popular frozen banquet cake, it was molded around a palisade of light lady fingers, filled with whipped egg whites, Bavarian cream and thick plum fruit puree. It was an extravagance to cook it for their small household, but Elanora felt like doing something rash. It seemed everyone but her was setting off on some new adventure. She needed to get some fun somehow.

Her thoughts were interrupted by the heavy thud of the brass door knocker. "Would you check on that, Aunt. I can't leave this — and Boston and father might not hear it."

Her aunt readily complied, and she set about the tricky business of piping the light sponge mixture onto the baking sheets ready for cooking, humming with quiet satisfaction as she went about her task.

Fourteen

Rafael was stamping his feet to warm up his toes when the door was opened by a stout middle-aged woman with penetrating blue eyes and gray hair covered in a black mantle. She opened her mouth to speak, but before she had a chance to greet him, a man's barking objection sounded from the hallway behind. She stepped aside as an elderly man in a wheelchair propelled himself to the door.

"Don't you see the wreath?" he snarled. "The house is in mourning. Visitors — particularly uninvited ones — are not welcome."

The woman attempted to intervene.

"Don't worry yourself, Henry, I can handle this."

"Go back to the kitchen, Gloria. This is my home." She shrugged and backed off. He glared up at Rafael. "So what is your business here? Spit it out."

Rafael began to explain who he was, and why he was here. He'd hoped to show Miss Elanora Travers some studio daguerreotypes he had taken, but if it was inconvenient he would be happy to return on another occasion.

As he spoke the old man's expression darkened, but he did not interrupt. When he'd completed his explanation, the old man backed his chair away from the door and gestured towards a doorway off the hall. Rafael stepped into the house and was immediately struck by a homely fragrance of vanilla, lemon and woodsmoke.

"In there," the old man said.

The woman had gone back down the corridor, and as she opened the door at the end of the hall the smell of vanilla grew stronger. Evidently the kitchen was in there. Rafael reluctantly went ahead into the drawing room. The old man followed and wheeled his chair past him. He gestured irritably to the door handle. "Close it."

When her aunt returned she brushed aside Elanora's inquiring look. "Someone for your father, I understand. He's dealing with it."

She picked up her embroidery and paused before putting her glasses back on. "Elanora, my dear, I've been thinking. How would you like to come and spend a few weeks with me in Brooklyn?

"You know I've got plenty of room, and Henry will be quite well taken care of here with Boston and Mrs O'Loughlin. Your sister might even put in an appearance if you aren't here to take care of everything. She is rather inclined to leave it all to you."

There was just the slightest hint of reproach in her voice. Elanora's much older sister Henrietta was married with five children and lived on a farm thirty miles up the Hudson River. She rarely visited, saying that New York was far too expensive for a poor country lawyer's wife.

The seven years that separated them in age was only part of the reason they'd never had much in common. Henrietta had adopted a very strict evangelical view and liked to regularly warn others of their sinful state and their need for salvation.

"Oh Aunt, she is so busy with the children. I understand."

She felt the hairs on the back of her neck prickle at the very mention. Henrietta was certainly the last person she wanted to meet in her current fragile state.

"But come home with you? I'd love that. Perhaps the simple change of air would do me good. I've felt low with what's been going on. I mean Connie and all."

Aunt Glory considered her over the top of her embroidery, glasses pushed down on her nose.

"Is Connie's death all that's bothering you, Elanora? Nothing else? You know you can always rely on me to keep a secret."

Elanora felt her cheeks reddening.

"A secret? I'm not sure what you

mean, Aunt." Her breath caught in her throat, and she knew she was blustering. Her aunt would not be fooled either. She snatched up the thick burlap oven cloth and stepped across to the stove to check on the sponge.

"Like what? Well, like that Miss Amelia Taylor. She's still a Miss, I presume. Tell me. Is she in the family way?"

Elanora had just opened the oven. As the shock of the casual inquiry registered, the oven cloth slipped, and her hand jabbed forward and touched the red-hot sponge tray.

"Ow!" She jumped back. "Ooh, I've burnt my hand. Botheration …"

Glory rose and poured a bowl of cold water from a jug on the bench. "Here. Sit down and put it in there to cool. You're not going to die." Her words were brusque, but her tone was soothing.

"Let me get the sponge fingers." She bent down. "They're looking perfect. Just the right straw color. You've done well." She drew out the heavy metal tray, set it to one side and closed the oven door.

"Sorry to shock you, Elanora, but I'm certain you know the answer to that last question. And I can see things aren't what they were between you and Eustace. So just what is going on?"

Elanora's eyes bolted to her Aunt's kindly face. "Oh no, Aunt, it's nothing like that. I mean to say … I don't know what you're implying."

Aunt Glory raised one eyebrow and gazed steadily at her without speaking.

She felt the sadness she had been trying to push down rise up in her, forcing its way through her chest, up into her throat, a tidal wave of unhappiness engulfing her.

"Oh, Aunt Glory. It's not what you're thinking." She took a great gulp of air. "It's much worse than you can imagine ..."

At first glance, the sitting room was pleasant but not luxurious

An old man's lair.

Two leather chairs sat either side of a glowing fire, one of them set ajar from the fireplace, with a half-read newspaper spread open on a side table beside it. Rafael selected the other and sat warily, sliding his image case in beside him.

Henry Travers — Rafael surmised the cantankerous old man was Elanora's father — pulled up his wheelchair alongside the newspaper-covered table and glared.

"So who are you again? Rafael who? And what do you want with my daughter?"

Rafael began his account once again, more slowly this time. He was an experienced portrait photographer, working with one of the most established daguerreotypists in New York, Mr Philip Haas. Mr Haas was the one who took the President's portrait, and he had some portraits of Miss Elanora Travers to show her.

"Sounds like a lot of nonsense to me," huffed Travers. He reached out and picked up a pipe from an ashtray buried under the newspaper. He fiddled in his jacket pocket for a match and lit the pipe while Rafael watched on in silence.

He drew a few puffs of smoke and then rested it in his lap and turned rheumy eyes on Rafael.

"I believe there has been some misunderstanding here. My daughter comes from one of the best families in

New York. If she has been consorting with some foreigner —" He spat the word and paused for another puff on the pipe — "Spanish did you say?" And continued. "Some photographer, then she should know better. But as her father I can tell you she is not receiving visitors like you, not today nor any other day. Reputation is not something to be squandered, and the Travers family's reputation is unsurpassed. You can pack up your goods and go."

Rafael remained erect and gracious in manner. "Forgive me, Mr Travers, the last thing I would want to do is cause offense. I wonder if you are aware that the very best of families are having their portraits done. I don't know if you have heard of Mathew Brady's Illustrious Americans?

"He's taking portraits of the most

prominent people. President Andrew Jackson, Judge Joseph Story, Edgar Allan Poe — they've all sat for portraits. I myself have had the honor of photographing Mrs Sarah Astor. I believe being seen this way can only enhance Miss Travers' reputation."

Henry Travers banged his pipe bowl on the edge of an earthenware ashtray with a force that spilled some of the hot charred contents into the tray.

"Mr Casta ... Casanova ... whoever you are. No Spanish photographer is going to be associated with any daughter of mine. Have I made myself clear? She has just turned twenty-one. She is about to be betrothed to a young man of very good family. And she will not be consorting with anyone of your ilk. Now kindly leave." He turned and pointed to the door. "You can let yourself out."

He glared for a long minute at Rafael, and then pointedly picked up the pipe and rustled the newspaper.

Rafael stood and glanced around the room, where the fruity smell of pipe smoke now mingled with the charcoal smell from the fire. A mantle clock kept strict time, tick tock, tick tock, and the fire randomly sparked. The old man ignored him.

He stepped away to the door, paused in the hallway and looked hopefully towards the closed kitchen door. Then he turned and went back out to his waiting hack.

Fifteen

She was ashamed to admit even to herself that she had opened the black velvet ring box every day since Eustace had given it to her on that birthday night and gazed down at the sparkling gem. Sometimes she put it on her finger before settling it back into the box.

But this morning, after her tearful talk with Aunt Glory in the kitchen yesterday, she had addressed a brown paper envelope to Eustace at the Mountfort mansion on Washington Square and had slipped the black box in it for Boston to deliver when he went on his morning errands for her father. She couldn't bring herself to include any note; it would be clear enough to

Eustace why she was returning it, without her having to say another word.

She hadn't told Glory the whole story — she was still hoping she'd be spared from having to do that — but she'd told her enough to leave her precious wearied face looking brooding and somber.

"William Mountfort always was a hard man," she said. "You've probably guessed theirs was never a love match. Connie's father was certain he was setting his daughter up to found a dynasty by joining together her inheritance and William's drive. And so it's turned out. The only thing that was missing was love and intimacy. Respect, perhaps. But not much love. I think William regards marrying Constance as one of his business triumphs — and he'll be obsessed about achieving a similar prize for Eustace.

"With Connie dead, I think you'll have to surrender any hopes of marrying Eustace my dear. I know William too well."

She'd been angered but not surprised by Amelia's state. "Men like William Mountfort can pretty well please themselves," she said.

"He enjoys the social status, but with the money he's got, he doesn't need it. And with the fortune he has, people are happy to act blind to his misbehavior. He might even get sneaking admiration for scoring a young beauty. My guess would be that Amelia will be installed as the new Mrs William Mountfort within the year."

The next morning Elanora waved Henry farewell and set out for a month-long stay with Glory. She felt hollow inside as she kissed his stubbly cheek and said her farewells, but a sense of relief washed over her as she stepped into the street. At least she wouldn't have to maintain her careful guard in front of him. She just prayed when she came back home she'd have nothing to hide.

Sixteen

Elanora's sense of carrying lesser cares didn't last long, even though spending time with Aunt Glory in her Brooklyn Heights cottage brought childhood memories of all their good times rushing back.

By the time she marched up the ramp at Ferry Landing she was reflecting anxiously on the knowledge that her monthly purge hadn't come like clockwork, as it usually did. It should be here by now.

She pushed the awareness to the back of her mind and desperately tried to focus on Aunt Glory's entertaining commentary about the rivalry between two local Irish bands who played evening concerts around town when the weather warmed up, embellishing her tales with anecdotes on the general liveliness of the city where she'd been principal of the girls' school for the past five years.

She was valiantly trying to divert Elanora's attention from her disappointment in love, but she only knew half the story. They established a companionable routine over the next few days, with her Aunt reporting to the school during the day while she amused herself reading, playing on a small piano in the front parlor, and strolling the back garden looking out for the tips of spring bulbs that were pushing up through the gradually warming soil.

In another few weeks or so the garden would be bright with snowdrops and the first daffodils. When her aunt came home they strolled together, taking coffee at one of the local houses. But always in the back of her mind was the gnawing anxiety: what would she do if she was with child?

She was playing some light classics in the parlor while her aunt worked on some school papers early one evening when there was a knock on the front door. She continued playing while her aunt got up to answer.

A minute or two later she returned, followed by a visitor. Elanora glanced up and her hands froze on the keyboard. Behind her aunt's stocky figure loomed a broad-shouldered man with a poet's aquiline profile and a shock of dark hair that curled loosely around his ears. In one hand he carried a black leather case. He paused in the doorway and smiled.

"Hello, Miss Travers. I've finally

tracked you down."

She slid off the piano stool and was grateful when her knees didn't buckle under her.

"Mr Castellanos …"

She glanced nervously toward her aunt. "Aunt Glory, this is Mr Rafael Castellanos." She licked her lips nervously and added, "The Spanish photographer who was engaged in taking my portrait before Aunt Coco died."

"I'm aware of Mr Castellanos. We've met before."

Her heart raced.

"Really? When was that?"

"At your father's. A day or so after Connie's funeral."

Elanora was stunned. She glanced in confusion from her aunt to Castellanos, caught completely off guard, not knowing what to say next. Her aunt moved aside and indicated an armchair near the piano.

"Mr Castellanos, why don't you take a seat and tell us what brings you to Brooklyn?"

Her aunt resumed her own seat and Elanora sank back down onto the piano bench.

"As Miss Travers mentioned, I am in the process of preparing some daguerreotype portraits of her to show in a Broadway gallery. We took the original studies just after Christmas but with the delays of the festive season and other unfortunate events I've been prevented from showing them to her until now. I am hoping you will allow me to present the work and give me approval to show them in an upcoming show at the Philip Haas Gallery."

He reached for the leather case he'd

placed on the floor beside him.

"I'm afraid that won't be possible." Elanora's voice sounded muted and strained even to her own ears. "My circumstances have changed. It would not be appropriate for a public display like that."

Rafael look up sharply and glanced across to her aunt. "I don't understand. There's really nothing controversial about them. Quite the opposite." He continued to unlatch the case. "Let me at least show you the results."

Elanora searched her aunt's face. "Is this acceptable to you Aunt? Really, I'll do whatever you recommend. You know what father's like."

"I see no harm in allowing Mr Castellanos to show us his work." Her aunt relaxed back in her chair. "I, for one, would be most interested to see it."

Rafael drew out the studies and laid them side by side on a long occasional table that ran along the wall under the windows. She and her aunt moved to the table and stared for a long time, neither of them speaking.

The young woman who stared up at her looked familiar — someone she had known a long time ago — but didn't really know anymore. Deep wistful eyes challenged the photographer's lens. The young woman was solemn, seeking, but there was a hint of mischief about the curve of her lips, a sense of energy and verve in the lifted eyebrow.

She looked assured of her place in the world; a young woman with a sure sense of who she was and where she belonged. Elanora let out a long breath. She was looking at a young woman who no longer existed.

She glanced across to her aunt and saw there were tears in her eyes. She dashed her hand across the corner of one of them, then the other, sniffed and smiled. "Sorry, my dear. I've got emotional. You look so beautiful. And so like your mother. It's all there, and it took me by surprise."

Rafael offered her an immaculately pressed white handkerchief with a light flourish. "A response from the heart, Senora. The best compliment anyone can give my work."

Her aunt took it with a weak smile. "Thank you."

"They are lovely, Rafael. Very fine work indeed. But the fact remains. I'm sorry, it's just not appropriate for them to be publicly shown."

Her aunt seemed to rally herself from her reverie. "Elanora, why don't we sit in the drawing room where there's more room and get some refreshments. I'd like to hear more of what Mr Castellanos has planned."

Seventeen

As Rafael backed out of the room, his hat in his hands, Elanora pressed her palms to her cheeks, as if the physical act of touching could reassure her that this meeting had really happened. He knew how she felt.

When he'd been turned away by her father's churlishness he'd tried to accept the rejection. It was a father's right to protect his daughter, he'd told himself, even if it was unreasonable. But he hadn't been able to forget her.

He stepped out of the house and the fresh cold air immediately brightened his cheeks and lightened his chest. When he reached the street, he stopped; he threw his head back and gazed up in wide-eyed wonder at the night sky, seeing it all with the eyes of his childhood.

A thin sliver of moon was visible to the west, its relative dimness allowing countless galaxies to shimmer overhead. He took a deep breath of harbor air and reached skyward with both hands, playing his old game of touching the stars. As a boy of eight or nine, he'd dreamed of traveling to far off places, and as a man he'd done that. Now he wanted expansion of a different kind.

He wanted the woman he'd just left behind in that stuffy parlor in his life forever. Even in the plain green day dress that said more clearly than anything that she wasn't inviting male attention, she cut straight to his heart. It came to him with a clarity and certainty that he'd only ever felt a few times before in his life. He couldn't, wouldn't walk away from her a second time.

He swung on his heel and walked down the hill to the village to find a cheap hotel for the night.

Eighteen

"You don't understand, Rafael. It's the American way." She squinted her eyes against the bright sun and her nose wrinkled so delightfully he wanted to reach out and touch it. "Well, the British way, I suppose, but we've made it our own with a vengeance."

She cleared her throat as if preparing for a public announcement. "The less often a woman is seen in public, the more highly she is esteemed." She shot him a quick smile and continued in a passable mimicking of a Master of Ceremonies' deep male voice. "Social rule number one hundred and ten."

Another wry smile. "According to one

of those etiquette guides being consulted by the smart set, anyway. And it seems my father's read them all."

When he'd returned to her aunt's home this morning she'd been all rugged up and ready to step out, saying that her aunt had given her permission to walk with him to the nearest coffee house, as long as they stayed in public view at all times. "You need something to cheer you up," her Aunt Glory had said.

Her cheeks were glowing from the cold. She was dressed for the weather, in a fur trimmed hooded cape in cherry red cashmere with a matching muff and black elastic-sided kid ankle boots. They had a table near the window in a popular Brooklyn coffee house and though the temperatures were still chilling, a weak late winter sun was breaking through.

He laughed and signaled to the waiter

to bring a fresh pot of coffee.

"Your father … You seem very patient with him. Is it difficult?"

The light pink flush he'd seen before when she was discomforted showed in her face. She cleared her throat and hesitated before replying.

"He's lost his way since my mother died. His health deteriorated so fast in the months after her death — and I think now he's an invalid shut away at home, he's losing touch. New York's changing so fast, and he just isn't keeping up. Maybe he even guesses that, though he won't admit it. So it's hard for him." She cast him an appeal for understanding.

"Is that a roundabout way of saying he's difficult?"

"Not difficult. Just stuck in his ways. And now his poor health is overtaking him. One thing's for sure. He'd never forgive me if he considered I'd shamed the family in any way. He's extremely sensitive about that. It's the only thing left that he can hold onto."

"And showing those portraits — that would shame the family?"

"Well, no one's really taking studies of women, are they? Plenty of important men, but no women. Father would never want to be a first in anything."

"Nonsense!" He leaned back in his chair and gave her an indulgent smile.

"All sorts of women are now having their portraits taken. Mrs Sarah Astor for starters, though I admit she hasn't allowed it to be shown in public. President's wives, famous singers like Jenny Lind, beautiful young French women — you know the process was developed in Paris don't you — character studies of older anonymous women proudly displaying their eye glasses. There is nothing disreputable in it at all.” He watched and waited while she sipped her coffee, and when she put the cup back down he leaned toward her.

“Elanora, have you ever asked yourself what you want from life?”

As soon as the question was out he wanted to swallow it back because she stiffened as if she’d been stung. She pulled back imperceptibly from the table, from him, spine rigid against the straight wooden back of her chair. Then she exhaled and seemed to concede something.

“Truth is, Mr Castellanos, there was only one thing I thought I wanted in life, and I’ve discovered I can’t have it.” She glanced at him and hastily looked away, back at the table, at her hands holding the handle of the cup.

"Am I permitted to ask what that one thing was?" He felt like a man venturing out on thin ice, unsure whether it would hold his weight or capsize under him.

She sat still and silent, her shoulders hunched forward, for what seemed like an eternity.

"The one thing I wanted was to marry my childhood sweetheart and live happily ever after. Naive, wasn't it?"

"Why naive?"

She shook her head. "I accuse my father of not understanding the changing rules, but I was blind to them myself. Everyone knows New Yorkers live and die by the marriage market.

"The merchant class likes to see themselves as self-made men, but take a close look at a roll call of the richest men downtown and you'll find pretty well all of them either got a start or substantially boosted their capital by marrying well.

"It's the New York game. And since my father's illness has incapacitated him to the point where he's of no economic benefit to an enterprise … Well, you can draw your own conclusions." Her mouth twisted into a brief bitter line. And then she gave a half laugh behind her hand, covering it.

He reached out and took her hand very gently in his own and held it. Her skin was warm and dry, and he could feel the gentle pulsing of her heart at her wrist.

"You could always elope?"

He wasn't sure whether he'd intended the remark as a wry defusing of her intensity or if he seriously meant to suggest it as an option. He was aware he was holding his breath as he searched her eyes.

"Elope?" The word came out jerky and sharp. She shook her head and began laughing. "Elope. Well there's just one problem with that. You need two willing participants." She glanced up at him and the bitterness had vanished. She was genuinely amused.

He let go of her hand and pushed the hair back out of his face.

"Any man who doesn't want to elope with you doesn't deserve you anyway."

Her merriment brightened further, her mouth falling open, revealing perfect white teeth, eyes sparkling.

"Oh, my dear Mr Castellanos, how very Spanish — how very romantic ..."

She'd taken the opportunity to turn the conversation into a joke, to slam the door shut on any further discussion of her life. He wasn't sure if he felt charmed or disappointed. He couldn't resist pushing one step further.

"Spanish and romantic? I plead guilty on both charges." He laughed along with her, and then he sobered. "But just tell me one thing. Say you did elope — what would your father do?"

"My father? He would shut the door on me and never open it again." The mirth faded from her eyes.

She made to push her chair away from the table. "I think it's time I went back home. I'm having far too much fun here for it to be good for my health."

She stood up and reached for the coat that she'd shed on the back of the chair as the room had warmed up.

He stood immediately and held it out for her, noticing as he did the way his heart beat quickened at the sight of her shining blond hair caught up at the back of her head, exposing the lovely vulnerable curve of her neck. He masked a sigh as he escorted her out into the watery sunshine.

Where are you going with this, Rafael Castellanos y Ordonez? Can't you see she's way out of your reach? This can only end badly.

Head and heart battled within him as he made the casual stroll up the hill back to Elanora's home.

As she unlocked the front door she turned to face him. "Oh, sorry, I forgot to mention. Aunt Glory says you are welcome to return for supper later, if you wish. She'd be happy to have a guest. It doesn't happen very often."

She gazed up at him with wide expectant eyes.

Yes really, it was no contest. His heart would win.

Nineteen

"My father is in town and would like to meet you."

Rafael had made no mention of his parents or his past life when he'd been at her aunt's for supper the previous evening, so the invitation came as a surprise.

"Oh? In town from where?"

"From Washington. He's a diplomat."

"Oh? A Spanish diplomat?" She knew she sounded dizzy, but he'd completely blindsided her with his casual revelation.

"That's right."

She giggled. "Sorry. I mean what else could he be?"

"Well, my mother is Scottish, so I

guess he could have been ... a Scottish diplomat?"

His eyes were twinkling with mischief.

"Rafael. You didn't say!" She held up her hands in a gesture of surrender.

"You didn't ask."

"And that's fair comment. So is he an ambassador?"

He nodded. "He's actually Spain's ambassador to Mexico. The war that's been going on the last few years has caused awful degradation and ruin, but I gather peace is about to be proclaimed. That's what brings Father to Washington, anyway. And why Mother isn't with him. She preferred not to travel this time."

Elanora nodded. "I see. And this meeting. When? And where? And should I be nervous?" It was her turn to tease.

"Dinner at the Rainbow Room."

Her stomach did a small flip. The last

time she'd been there was for her birthday. Everyone who was anyone wanted a table there, and if William and Eustace were out and about, there was a chance they'd be eating there. But what did that matter? She was nothing to them, right? And anyway, Eustace was already on his way to the Indies, having had his trip already delayed once by his mother's death. He had to be.

"Oh goodness. I might just have to go home to collect an evening gown. I don't think I brought anything suitable for the Rainbow Room with me. I wasn't expecting to go anywhere so grand."

"Just look your normal understated beautiful self, that's all that's required. Don't worry. He'll love you."

Twenty

"Miss Elanora Travers, meet my father, Marqués Angel de Castellanos y Ordonez."

She was as ready as she ever would be. In deference to Coco she was in 'half mourning' in a high-necked grey silk trimmed in black lace layers down the full skirt. The nipped-in waist felt tight tonight, and she thought uncomfortably of Amelia in Trinity church on Christmas Eve.

Elanora bobbed a quick courtesy and extended her right hand. "Delighted to meet you, Marqués."

He was a head shorter than Rafael, a stout barrel of a man in comparison to his willowy, athletic son, sporting a smoothly trimmed dark beard and a black evening cape. His eyes were piercing, and he had a presence and authority unmatched by any other man in the room.

In the first few intense seconds after she sat down, she sensed he was gauging her mettle, but she didn't feel uncomfortable under the silent interrogation.

"A very beautiful dress, Senorita. I am glad to see Rafael has such good taste."

His mouth quirked up at one corner, and she realized he was having a joke at Rafael's expense. He turned to his offspring and said, "And you, my son. How is the art of the daguerreotype progressing?"

Rafael leaned in to Elanora. "Father is quite a virtuoso with the camera himself

— and mostly self-taught."

The senior Castellanos waved away his comment and turned his attention to the table.

"I think it's a night for champagne, Senorita. Do you drink champagne?"

Elanora nodded politely. "Sounds lovely. Thank you."

They'd been ushered into a red leather banquette she suspected was reserved for special guests, positioned so it overlooked the main dining floor. She could see heads turning as they were seated, curious diners contorting themselves to check out who'd arrived. They'd be disappointed it wasn't a Vanderbilt or an Astor, or at least someone they recognized.

She sat on high alert, trying to put it all together.

First, she'd belatedly discovered

Rafael's father was a diplomat. Now she'd learned he was also a Marqués. Elanora's stomach was queasy. That was some family heritage.

Rafael had deliberately let her — and her father — think he was an itinerant photographer of no particular means, hadn't he? Or was it their fault for not paying more attention, for not asking the right questions?

Her cheeks burned as she recollected Glory's account of Henry's brusque dismissal. She hadn't been there to witness it, but she cringed at the likely exchange. It was amazing Rafael had even bothered to come back.

The sick feeling worsened. If anyone was a fraud here, it was her, presenting herself like she was an innocent maiden when she was really spoiled goods. She looked across the table to the Marqués and his son, heads leaned in close as they happily chatted about some technical point of photography while the waiter poured the champagne.

"Forgive us, Miss Travers, it's been a while since we had a chance to talk, and I always enjoy hearing about Rafael's latest techniques. That's one of the wonderful things about photography — there's always something new to learn. He tells me you met through the gallery?"

The memory of that afternoon, of the devastating confrontation with Eustace and her final realization he was too weak to ever stand up to his father, deepened her nausea. She felt hot, clammy. She pulled her scrambled thoughts together.

"Yes, that's right. Quite by chance really. I'd never been there before — I'd just got separated from friends in the

Christmas shopping crowds and wandered down a side lane and there it was!"

She smiled at the two men who were regarding her with slightly concerned looks from the other side of the table.

They might differ in their physique, but Rafael was stamped with his father's dark good looks and sparking intelligence. She wondered what his mother was like, and then was almost immediately glad she wasn't here. Another woman would probably pick up what an impostor she was at first glance.

"Are you feeling alright, Miss Travers? Is the temperature in here to your liking?" Marqués Angel de Castellanos was looking at her like a concerned father, eyebrows raised into two lined furrows along his forehead.

"I was feeling a little lightheaded, but

I'm fine now," she said, sounding more confident than she felt. "Perhaps I'd better go easy on the champagne."

She flashed a smile at Rafael and was relieved to see him relax back into his seat with an appreciative answering gleam in his eye.

"I've done some wonderful studies of Elanora. I'm just trying to convince her to allow them to be shown publicly."

"Oh?" said the Marqués with a note of curiosity. "I have a lot to learn about America. Why do you need persuading? Your presidents, your generals, they are all happy to be displayed, yes? So what is the problem?"

Elanora felt at a loss as to what to reply. She shrugged. "I suppose … My father, he doesn't like the idea of his daughter hung on a gallery wall."

"Ah, I see, a proud father. I don't

blame him. A beautiful daughter like you, he wants to take good care of her."

Angel Castellanos smiled indulgently and picked up the menu. "I can tell you, it is very unusual for my son to invite me to meet young ladies of his acquaintance. You must be very special."

He looked affectionately towards Rafael. "Now, perhaps we should order? Do you like oysters, Miss Travers?"

She didn't like oysters, and that lack of taste seemed to her another breadcrumb, another marker on the shadowed trail that was beckoning her away from any thought of a future with this charming man.

What was I thinking? Her head spun with self-recrimination. *I'm sitting here pretending everything is fine and dandy when I'm possibly — maybe even probably — carrying another man's child.*

What would they think of me if they knew?

As dinner progressed she summoned up all the reserves within her to play-act her part; the vivacious, gracious young woman out to dinner with her charming beau and his illustrious father. Tournedos of filet of beef, roast canvasback duck, aubergine fritters, followed by tortoni and meringue glace. But as the dessert plates were cleared, she was teetering dangerously close to misery.

As she faded into silence, Rafael entertained his father with lively chatter of petty rivalries and new processes, and his father answered with news of his mother Fanny and the younger children.

"We've not been too badly affected by the war in Santa Fe," he explained. "But once the peace is signed, the capital will have to move back down south, of course. I don't think your mother is too happy about that. They've had a much harder time down there than we have. Mexico City's been devastated."

Rafael glanced over to Elanora. "I think we need to leave soon, Father. I'm not sure Elanora is quite her usual self, even though she reassured us earlier she was fine." He let the words fall away gently, a note of concern in his voice.

She gave a wan smile. "I'm sorry. I have been feeling a little odd, but it hasn't spoilt my enjoyment. I've had a wonderful time. I do thank you so much for your hospitality, Marqués."

"You're welcome, young lady. Anyone who's a friend of Rafael's is a friend of mine."

Their ride home was made in silence, and at her father's front door she turned to thank him. "Sorry I was such a sad sack tonight. I don't know what got into me."

He gazed down at her, his eyes liquid. "I'm sorry you aren't well, but don't worry, Father was still charmed."

"Rafael …" Her voice caught as she began. "It was a lovely evening. Really. And I feel privileged to have met your father. But I think perhaps it's best if we don't continue with this … friendship.

She paused and steeled herself. "I think it's best if we don't see one another again."

There. She'd done it. The right thing.

He took a step back and gazed down at her, his expression serene as he read her face. Then he stepped in close again and cupped one side of her face gently in his hand.

"Don't be ridiculous, Mia Cara."

He bent down and kissed her, the

softest, gentlest caressing of lips. Light, fluttery to the touch, but magnetic. She wanted it to go on forever, for her never to have to separate from the charge that flowed between them. Instant loss hit her when he stepped away, just as calmly as he'd stepped forward.

"I will call for you at ten tomorrow. Until then, mia hermosa dama — my beautiful lady — sleep well."

Twenty-One

"What was wrong last night? Something was bothering you. And you seem absolutely fine today."

They were sitting in the Castle Gardens, well wrapped up against the fresh wind, a morning coffee snack spread out before them. She had the hood up on her cashmere cape and the fur trim tickled as she ducked her head. She owed him an explanation, but that didn't make it any easier.

"Rafael, you're very special to me. I realized just how special when I saw you with your father last night. I feel honored to have been introduced to your family circle, I really do … But I can't go any further with it. I just can't."

The fine lines around his eyes tightened. She sensed he was holding himself back from reacting strongly to her words.

"Just can't? Why not? Forgive me if I am so indelicate as to suggest you didn't seem to object to me kissing you last night. In fact, I suspect you rather liked it. Liked it a lot."

He gave her a dark sultry look which suggested he'd consider repeating the act right here if it weren't such a public place, and her heart fluttered like a butterfly resting on marigolds.

She blushed and chewed her lip. "I did, Rafael. Be sure, I did. But that doesn't change anything."

He frowned, and for the first time a muscle in his cheek flexed.

"What is wrong, for goodness sakes.

Just come out and tell me; Is it your father?"

She shook her head. "You recall when we first met — was that only three weeks ago — you described me as 'lovelorn' or some such? And yes, I'd had a romantic disappointment. I was running away from an argument the night we met." She took a deep breath. "Well, I've been very stupid, Rafael. I've done the one thing everyone says a girl should not do …"

He looked wary, but reached out and gently took one of her hands in his. "Go on. I am listening."

She gazed at him, unsure of how to continue.

Nothing for it but to get it out there.

"Eustace was my childhood sweetheart. I thought we'd be together and he did too. He asked me to marry him. He even gave me an engagement ring on my twenty-first birthday. And I thought ... I thought we were going to be together forever."

She pulled her hand away from his and linked both hands protectively across her stomach, hugging herself for courage.

As he gazed at her with those liquid eyes that made her want to melt into him, she saw an awareness light up in them.

"Mia Cara. You are saying you are — as we say — la palomito sucia — a little soiled dove?"

She nodded, and a tear slid down her cheek. She dashed it away.

"Yes. Yes, that's what I am saying. Una palomito sucia. And I felt such a fraud sitting there with you and you father last night. I didn't deserve to be there ..."

Rafael looked around him. His finely shaped brows were contracted, his eyes solemn.

"Ah Elanora, I wish I could take you in my arms right now and show you this revelation changes nothing for me." He cast his hands out, palms open. "To save you embarrassment, I won't do it. But I want to." He laughed. "You might think we Spaniards are what, feudal, in our attitude to women?"

She shook her head. "No, no, not feudal. But even in America — well it's not acceptable."

"Elanora, you'd be surprised. We're more enlightened that you might think. And as for me. Well, I don't want a life without you.

"That's one reason I wanted Father to meet you last night. He understood. I want you to be my wife, and from what you've just been telling me, I don't think we should waste any more time."

The tears were flowing down both cheeks now. She stared at him with wide-eyed disbelief, and then flung her arms around his neck and sobbed into his shoulder.

"Rafael, I just can't believe ..." The rest of her words were drowned out by her convulsive weeping.

She'd dried her eyes. They sparkled back at him as she said that 'Yes, yes, she would adore to become the first — and she hoped the only — Mrs Rafael Castellanos y Ordonez'. He'd returned her to her Aunt Glory's house while he retraced his steps to Henry Travers' Bleecker Street parlor.

He braced himself for a frigid reception, and it was just as well he did.

The old man was adamant. No Spanish photographer was going to marry his daughter. Ever. He didn't get to explain about his family's status and accomplishments, and it didn't matter. He suspected it wouldn't have made any difference to the old man's dogmatic views.

He walked away thanking God that Elanora had reached her majority and didn't need his permission anyway. He'd arrange for a friend to take a daguerreotype of the occasion and they'd send it to him later.

Epilogue

On a fine February day with the air full of the fragrance of wedding bouquet daffodils Elanora Grayson Travers and Rafael Castellanos y Ordonez were married in a simple ceremony at St Paul's Chapel, Broadway.

The bride wore a sparkling gown in a French design from Stewart's Marble Palace store. The *New York Tribune* item the next day noted that the witnesses for the occasion were the groom's father, the Spanish ambassador to Mexico, the Marqués Angel de Castellanos y Ordonez, and the bride's aunt, Miss Gloria Grayson, a well-known New York educator.

The day was captured on daguerreotype by one the Mr Castellanos' friends, the celebrated society photographer Mathew Brady. It was believed the newlyweds were to honeymoon in Central America, after visiting the groom's mother, the Marquésa Fanny de Castellanos y Ordonez, in Santa Fe, New Mexico.

Amelia Taylor and William Mountfort were married in a private ceremony in Paris in June, 1848. Amelia had lost her first child three months into the pregnancy but she and William went on to have five sturdy boys who were all raised to excel at commerce.

Eustace never married, and as Rafael had predicted, bitterly regretted his whole life that he'd not wed Elanora as a young man.

Six months after Elanora and Rafael wed, in August 1848, in Nicaragua, where they were holidaying with Marquésa Fanny de Castellanos y Ordonez, Elanora was delivered of a lusty-lunged daughter she named Grayson Castellanos, in honor of her Aunt Glory, who had stood by her through her darkest days.

She'd been determined to name the child Grayson, whether it was a boy or a girl, because she said without her aunt's wise counsel, she'd never have found a way to marry Rafael, who truly was the love of her life.

As for Grayson? She was a strong-willed little tot who was always known as Graysie. From birth, she had unusually long slender fingers. The fingers of an artist, they said, and Rafael always joked that she was going to be a photographer, just like him.

THE END

Coming Soon
Unbridled Vengeance, Book Five, Of
Gold & Blood.

Bloodstained land. Harrowing
secrets. Can a wrongly accused
rancher solve a brutal crime before
he's locked away forever?

Rural Sacramento, 1870. Nathan Stewart can't wait to be a family man. After battling natural disasters and legal challenges to secure his land claim, he's finally free to court the French beauty next door.

Madeline Laurent hopes a fresh start in America will help her forget painful memories. But even though her homicidal husband fled and vanished, she's still legally bound to a man who's likely dead.

Want to read more of Unbridled Vengeance? The first four chapters are available for FREE. Download at https://www.jennywheeler.biz/tangled-destiny-free-chapters/

Enjoy This Book?

You can make a difference...

Reviews are the most powerful means for an author like me to get attention for my books. Much as I'd like to, I don't have the reach of a New York publisher, and bill boards and full-page advertising are way beyond my budget.

But I do have something much more powerful and effective than that, and it's something those publishers would kill for:

A committed and loyal bunch of readers.

Honest reviews of my books help bring them to the attention of other readers.

If you enjoyed this book I would be grateful if you could spend just a few minutes leaving a review wherever you can.

Post Your Reviews Here:
For Amazon:
http://geni.us/TangledDestiny
For Goodreads: https://bit.ly/30p3rUu

Thank you very much!

ACKNOWLEDGMENTS

Wishing everyone a very happy Christmas to round off what has been an amazing year, with the first four books — and the first Book Bundle of Books 1–3 — published in the last six months. (Of course, writing them took a lot longer than that.)

I would once again like to thank the librarians — particularly at Auckland Central and my own local Birkenhead Library — for their patient help and support with locating sometimes difficult to access research material and helping manage my prodigious borrowing, not just for the books, but also for all the

Joys of Binge Reading podcast interviews (www.thejoysofbingereading.com) I've done as well.

I have had such a lot of positive comments on the cover designs for all of the *Of Gold & Blood* books and *Tangled Destiny* is no exception. Award-winning designer Jane Dixon-Smith at JD Smith Design (http://www.jdsmith-design.com/) has shown an unerring eye all the way through, and I have been delighted with the results, as have readers. Whenever I look at the books together I am grateful to her for her work.

Once again Marina and Jason at Polgarus Studio (https://www.polgarusstudio.com/) have been stalwarts who are completely reliable in helping set the nuts and bolts of publishing in place.

And I would never have survived the post-publication without the marvellous assistance I have from graphic designer and web assistant Jo Cheong, who has worked wonders from her Singapore home office.

Nikki Crutchley at Crucial Corrections (https://www.crucialcorrections.co.nz/) once again gave valiant proofreading support under severe time constraints.

And as usual, any mistakes are wholly my responsibility. With the best will in the world little things seem to slip through, and I apologise in advance if that occurs this time.

God willing, there will be more *Of Gold & Blood* stories coming, but in the meantime I hope we are all going to enjoy a restorative Christmas break — and if you happen to be reading one of the books in the series, let me know what you think at jenny@jennywheeler.biz!

Happy Christmas everyone!

Jenny

ABOUT THE AUTHOR

Jenny Wheeler is the author of the Of Gold & Blood Old California mystery series:

Poisoned Legacy #1.
Brother Betrayed #2.
Double Jeopardy #3.
Tangled Destiny #4 (Christmas novella and Prequel.)
Unbridled Vengeance #5
Hope Redeemed #6
Tainted Fortune Book #7

Boxed Set/Book Bundle Of Gold & Blood, Series 1 Books 1 – 3.
Boxed Set/ Book Bundle Of Gold & Blood Series 2 Books 1 & 4

Jenny's online home is at
jennywheeler.biz or email
Jenny@jennywheeler.biz

You can connect with Jenny on:
Facebook: @JennyWheeler.Biz
Twitter: @Jenny_Biz
Instagram: @jennysbingereading
Pinterest
www.pinterest.nz/Jennywheelerbooks

www.ingramcontent.com/pod-product-compliance
Lightning Source LLC
Chambersburg PA
CBHW070457200726
48293CB00007B/2248